...your assistance."

Bella looked him over critically. "I daresay you are considered quite a prize. I have decided you are exactly what I need."

Dysart was shaken indeed. "Here, now—I say—I have no wish to be caught in the parson's mousetrap!"

She tapped a foot, annoyed. "Who has said anything about marriage?"

Dysart wet his lips. "You must be aware of my aunts' intentions. You cannot blame me for—for being concerned."

"Believe me, marriage to you is not in my plans. I want you for quite another thing. How are you at seducing females?"

"I—I beg your pardon?"

"I want you to lure that red-haired woman away from Chesney, so..." She slipped her arms around the startled earl's neck. "I accept the offer you are about to make."

## Books by Winifred Witton

**HARLEQUIN REGENCY ROMANCE**
46–LADY ELMIRA'S EMERALD
54–THE DENVILLE DIAMOND
74–THE MASKED MARQUIS

Don't miss any of our special offers. Write to us at the following address for information on our newest releases.

Harlequin Reader Service
P.O. Box 1397, Buffalo, NY 14240
Canadian address: P.O. Box 603,
Fort Erie, Ont. L2A 5X3

# THE SPECTRE OF SPADEFIELD

## WINIFRED WITTON

*Harlequin Books*

TORONTO • NEW YORK • LONDON
AMSTERDAM • PARIS • SYDNEY • HAMBURG
STOCKHOLM • ATHENS • TOKYO • MILAN
MADRID • WARSAW • BUDAPEST • AUCKLAND

If you purchased this book without a cover you should be aware that this book is stolen property. It was reported as "unsold and destroyed" to the publisher, and neither the author nor the publisher has received any payment for this "stripped book."

For Janice, who took me into the family business

Published December 1992

ISBN 0-373-31188-5

THE SPECTRE OF SPADEFIELD

Copyright © 1992 by Winifred Witton Smith. All rights reserved. Except for use in any review, the reproduction or utilization of this work in whole or in part in any form by any electronic, mechanical or other means, now known or hereafter invented, including xerography, photocopying and recording, or in any information storage or retrieval system, is forbidden without the permission of the publisher, Harlequin Enterprises Limited, 225 Duncan Mill Road, Don Mills, Ontario, Canada M3B 3K9.

All the characters in this book have no existence outside the imagination of the author and have no relation whatsoever to anyone bearing the same name or names. They are not even distantly inspired by any individual known or unknown to the author, and all the incidents are pure invention.

The Harlequin trademarks, consisting of the words HARLEQUIN REGENCY ROMANCE and the portrayal of a Harlequin, are trademarks of Harlequin Enterprises Limited; the portrayal of a Harlequin is registered in the United States Patent and Trademark Office and in the Canada Trade Marks Office.

Printed in U.S.A.

# CHAPTER ONE

THIRTEEN MINUTES BEFORE midnight, and on the outskirts of fashionable London, a full moon cast its glow over Spadefield House, the ancestral home of the Westphales. Clad in a wine velvet doublet, Parsifal, the first Earl of Spadefield, hefted a heavy sack over his shoulder, a pulsing illumination emanating from his nebulous form. His figure was not tall, and as he mounted the curving staircase from the Great Hall, his too-long sword got stuck on a step and tangled between his legs. It tripped him and his aura turned blue with a spectral curse. Reaching the Grand Ballroom, on the second floor, he crossed with measured tread to the wall adjoining the West Tower. He dissolved through it and disappeared.

In the bookroom below, Dysart Gregory Sylvester Westphale, the sixth Earl of Spadefield, stretched his legs towards the only hearth he could afford to keep lit. In spite of the impeccable fit of his coat of blue superfine, owing—and owed—to the hands of Weston, the superb polish of his gleaming Hessians, and the careful tousling of his wavy butter-coloured hair, there hung about him a subtly rakish air, bordering on the disreputable. A slight frown creased youthful features already marked by dissipation.

"Gadzooks, zounds and i' faith," he remarked irreverently. "The Old Gentleman sounds unhappy tonight." He extended an exquisitely shod toe and stamped out a spark that threatened to ignite the threadbare Aubusson carpet.

Across from him, his paternal aunt, Lady Eglantine Westphale, humphed and shook her grey curls. "So he should be." She sniffed.

On the opposite side of the hearth, her twin sister Lady Almeria, raised her elegant, turbaned head from her needlework. "Are not we all? Who wouldn't be unhappy when about to lose one's ancestral home?"

"Oh, as for that," said Lady Eglantine. "*He'll* stay. And may he terrify that dratted Thorpington out of his black little mind."

"Think you he'll drive him to Bedlam?" Lady Almeria asked hopefully.

"Wouldn't do us a penn'orth of good if he did." Dysart attempted a cheerful grin. "Before he'd get the chance, we'd have to be out."

Lady Eg grunted as she bent forward in her chair to scratch the tummy of a snoring pug. "Encroaching windsucker," she muttered. She gave equal attention to another little dog, who wriggled its rear ecstatically in lieu of wagging a totally inadequate tail. "Thorpington will bring us to fiddlestick's end."

"Our creditors will, my dear. Thorpington is merely their tool of destruction."

"Be that as it may, I cannot but feel it is somehow his fault we face utter ruination."

The sixth earl shook his head. "We shall come about, ducks. We always have."

There was a singular sweetness in Dysart's smile as he observed his maiden aunts. No twins could be less alike—or more in tune with each other. Lady Almeria, the eldest by nearly twenty minutes, was an aristocrat to her slender fingertips. Lady Eglantine, short and round, bred pugs and resembled one.

She raised a lugubrious face, like a pup refused a juicy bone. "Is there no way to keep Spadefield House from falling into Thorpington's hands?"

Lady Almeria stabbed a stitch into the firescreen she was repairing, nearly rending the fabric. "Once our home goes on the block, we have no say as to its purchaser."

Spadefield House, the ancient estate of six generations of earls, was about to be sold for debts, not only those of Dysart, the current earl, but also those of his expensive aunts and the five previous impecunious earls. And Eustace Thorpington, a distant cousin and festering thorn in the Westphales' sides, would be that buyer. Not only did he have what amounted to a bottomless purse, his father having married the daughter of a wealthy East India nabob, but as matters now stood, he was Dysart's heir. That last might change, but one way or another,

Eustace Thorpington intended to be the master of Spadefield.

And the possessor of Parsifal's lost treasure.

TWENTY MILES AWAY, an informal hop was taking place at the country estate of Viscount Robisham. The light from two chandeliers, each holding fifty tapers, glittered on gilded rout chairs and on the best jewels and satin of the cream of county society. Two drawing-rooms, combined into one by the opening of the wide double doors between them, accommodated six sets of four dancers. The settees had been removed, the carpets rolled away and the twenty-foot-tall rose brocade draperies pulled aside from the open French doors to catch an errant breeze, for country dancing made warm work.

Mr. Chesney Carlyle, his hand lightly resting at her waist, steered Lady Isabella Greenlea, the viscount's daughter, out through one of the French doors onto the balcony. She gazed up at him, her eyes adoring, for he was a romantically handsome gentleman, above medium height, with the athletic build of a Corinthian and the sultry, dark visage of a Byron. Resplendent in his Town evening attire, he cast the local squires into the shade. It was sometimes hard for Isabella to remember he was local himself, the son of Sir Arthur Carlyle, Robisham's nearest neighbour, and she had known him all her life.

That was her problem. While willing to do the pretty by the little daughter of his father's friend and stand up with her at dances, Ches was not about to offer for her hand.

Moonlight flooded the park below the balcony, shimmering on the ornamental lake. A gentle breeze rippled the leaves of the elm tree on their left and carried up the fragrance from the rose garden. The situation couldn't be better. His hand still rested on her waist; if she turned and swayed gently against him, his arm would be about her.

An accomplished ladies' man, Chesney Carlyle had not wasted his three years in Town. He knew what to do when alone in the moonlight with a damsel who held up her face, puckered her lips and closed her eyes. Before he thought, he did it.

It was, perhaps, the shortest kiss of his career.

He pushed her away. "Dammit, Bella, what the devil are you up to? You can't go about kissing men on balconies!"

"I wasn't kissing men. I was only kissing you."

"Well, I am a man and it is not at all the thing for a chit like you."

"*You* kissed *me*, Ches," Lady Isabella reminded him.

"That's nothing to do with the matter! You asked for it."

"I know. Did I not do it well? I thought," she explained artlessly, "I would practice on you."

"Practice!"

"Although it is not as if I have not kissed anyone before. I kissed Tommie Gooden once."

He frowned. "I remember. You told me. But you were only twelve and I boxed your ears."

"Are you going to box them again?" she asked, interested.

"Of course not! Bella, if you must practice your feminine wiles, you are right to work them on me. You are safe with me, but do not, for God's sake, try this with any other man!"

There it was. She was *safe* with Chesney Carlyle.

"How else am I to learn how to go on?" she demanded.

"Not that way!" He threw up his hands, helpless. "Bella, if this is not just like you. You have no more decorum than a school-room miss! I daresay," he added severely, "you have been reading novels again. When will you grow up?"

She stamped her foot, not producing a proper sound with her satin slipper. "I *am* grown up. I am now eighteen and I must learn to flirt so I can catch a husband."

A sudden silence fell thick between them. She made a tentative try to cut her way through it. Trailing a finger along the balcony rail, she looked down at it as though it were the most important thing in the world. "I plan to become betrothed in the very near future."

"Really," said Chesney Carlyle. "And whom do you intend to marry?"

Didn't he know? How could he be so obtuse? Annoyed, Lady Isabella tried another tack. "I am to leave for London almost at once, Ches. My father has written to Lady Almeria Westphale, who is my godmother, to ask that she sponsor my come-out this Season. I mean to be betrothed before I go."

"That is perfectly ridiculous. My dear girl, the whole purpose of a London Season is to contract a suitable alliance."

"Oh, indeed? Can you not see my point? I am being sent to Town like a prize heifer to an agricultural fair! To be sold to the highest bidder!"

"Bella, you must not speak so. It is most unbecoming in you. The idea is to present you to Society as a well-bred young lady, not as a hurly-burly miss on the catch for the most eligible man. Indeed, I agree with your father. Going to London will be just the thing. You've become too devilish attractive to settle for some country bumpkin. Why, with your beauty you may even become a duchess."

This was exactly *not* what Isabella wished him to say. Why couldn't he see that what she really wanted was not a duke but a certain future baronet?

She began to feel uneasy. Ches had not responded at all as he should have. In fact, of late he had seemed almost formal and distant, not like the familiar elder brother figure she had always known. For an instant, her heart went cold. She knew of a possible reason. She should have taken more seriously the tale brought to her by her abigail who was "walking out" with Chesney's valet.

According to the domestics, always *au courant* of the affairs of their betters, Mr. Chesney Carlyle had a new light o' love in Town and the "lady" in question was no such thing. An opera dancer from Covent Garden, her abigail reported. A statuesque female with dark eyes and raven hair. Bella was petite and fair with bright blue eyes that began to glint with determination. Females of that sort had naught to do with a gentleman's marriage, nor should they.

She was quite in favour of Ches's being enamoured, but with herself, for at the age of fourteen, she had fallen madly in love with him when he came home from Oxford. She decided then he was the man she'd marry and she still intended to do so, for she had long suspected he was not entirely indifferent to her. It was only his silly code of honour that kept him, a lowly baronet's son, from offering for one he believed ranked far above him. Well, she might be able to shorten that distance.

Before she lost her nerve, Bella cast all her chips in a single throw.

"Ches, if I am not to be wed to a country bumpkin, what about to yourself?"

"Me! Good God, Izzy!" he exclaimed, the power of his emotion betrayed by his reverting to her near-forgotten childhood nickname. "I've never heard so impossible a suggestion in my life!"

"Why not?" she blurted. "I have no wish to be a duchess."

"Izzy," he began carefully, "you are talking absolute fustian. I am no more a suitable match for a lady of your rank than... than the vicar... or... or your father's bailiff."

"How can you say so? It is you who is being nonsensical!"

He looked down at her, catching her shoulders to turn her towards him. "Bella, your father would be the first to agree with me. In no way can I, once removed from a commoner, aspire to the hand of a viscount's daughter."

"That is *your* father speaking, not mine! Sir Arthur is a top-lofty prig."

His lips thinned and he remained silent. His arm went round her again, but only to lead her back into the house. That was it. She had done her best. Obviously, it would take stronger measures to convince Mr. Chesney Carlyle he was the only man for her, and the first step was to go to Town. When she had turned down the offers of the most eligible men in the Metropolis, perhaps then he would realize that the rural maid with whom he grew up had no desire to throw her cap at a great title.

MR. CHESNEY CARLYLE DROVE home at the close of the evening, prey to troublesome thoughts. He knew of Bella's childhood infatuation for him and had been trying to counteract it. Obviously, without success. She might even believe she had conceived a lasting passion. And that, in all honour, he could not permit. His father, too, was aware of Bella's transparent adoration and continually dinned into his son his fears that Ches would develop a tendre for the girl and encourage her, which would not do. Naturally, Ches was fond of young Bella, but he knew his place—only too well, thanks to Sir Arthur Carlyle.

Irritably, he flicked his whip above his pair. A gentleman did not raise hopes he was in no position to fulfil in the breast of an innocent maiden. He did not need to be constantly reminded. With her undeniable beauty, Lady Isabella Greenlea could look as high as she wished for a *parti*. It would be the work of a curst rum touch to take advantage of her innocence—even if he wished to do so. Immured in the country as she was, she had known few men, the sons of country squires, the older friends of her father's—and himself.

He had been acquainted with Isabella all her life, having been allowed, at the responsible age of seven, to peek into the cradle of a pink-and-white cherub wrapped in lace and ribbons. Even then he had thought her beautiful. Tonight, at eighteen, she had taken his breath away.

She had kissed him. He could still feel her soft, slender body in his arms...the fragrance of her scent prickled in his nostrils...she was lovely in the moonlight.... She *had* grown up!

His mind continued to dwell on her charms as he drove, but she was *not* for him. His father would comb his hair with a joint stool for even thinking so of her!

She *should* go to London and have her chance, but he felt some trepidation. She was a green girl, no matter what she thought, not at all up to snuff and by far too impulsive. He felt responsible for her, owing to her childish attachment to him. There was no knowing what ineligible fortune-hunter or half-pay officer she might fix her heart upon next. He'd best take a hand in selecting a proper husband for Lady Isabella Greenlea.

As soon as he was back in his chambers, he sat down at his writing desk and trimmed a quill. With painstaking care, he made out a list of the qualifications of a *parti* for Isabella.

First of all: His rank must be equal to hers. That eliminated himself. He was out of the running at the post. Second: impeccable lineage, naturally; number three: unquestionable honour; four: wealth, equal to her own; five: he must be a man of fashion. A dandified coxcomb would not do. Which brought up number six: consequence. He must be of the utmost respectability.

Number seven: disposition, even tempered, agreeable; and number eight: intelligent. One of Bella's volatile nature would never put up with a fool.

Ches tickled his chin with the feather end of his quill. What else? Ah, number nine: the man must be presentable as to face and figure. An ill-looking personage would never appeal to Bella.

He read over what he had written, carefully. A long list, perhaps, but it was best to consider all essentials. His methodical mind felt there should be an even ten points, but he couldn't, at the moment, think of another.

He had a sudden sobering thought that sent him, post-haste, to pay her a visit the next day.

"Bella," he began at once, "did you not say the name of your godmother is Westphale?"

To his dismay, she assured him it was.

"But that is the family of the Earl of Spadefield!" Chesney knew something of the rackety earl. The man had an unsavoury reputation. "You don't want to go there," he said flatly.

Isabella, having spent a good part of the night in considering their conversation of the evening before, was in no mood to look favourably upon him. "Yes, I do," she said.

Chesney hesitated. How could he explain? Some aspects of the sixth earl's way of life were not matters a gentleman might discuss with a delicately nurtured young lady. The tale of Lord Spadefield's *affaire de coeur* with a titled lady nearly twice his age still drew awed comment in the clubs. None of this could he mention to Bella. His innate sense of honour would not permit him to sully her tender ears.

He said instead, "His lordship is one who has gone his length in every extravagant folly. I feel certain you could not wish to make his acquaintance."

"I am visiting my godmother," she told him, her lips tight. "Not your disagreeable earl."

Ah, an opening. "That is my point." Ches spoke up quickly. "In company, he is not at all disagreeable. I fear he is quite the opposite, one who is by far too personable, as well favoured as he is charming."

Bella shrugged a dainty shoulder. "I daresay I'll not see much of him."

Chesney took a turn about the room, frowning. "The man is not cast out of Society. You may meet him everywhere, but he is known to be a here-and-therian."

She peeked at him sideways, a mischievous twinkle in her eyes. "Indeed? I have never met such a one. Perhaps I should *cultivate* his acquaintance."

This was what he feared. "You speak flummery, my girl. The man will have wiles you know naught of. He is an expert in the art of dalliance and you are but the greenest of girls."

"I am not!" she flared. "And in any case, it is to his *aunts* I go—unless you disapprove of them, as well?"

"No, no, of course not." He had met Lady Almeria once at a rout and retained a vague memory of an elderly, fragile-appearing aristocrat. "Lady Almeria Westphale's reputation is impeccable, and there is naught against her sister, Lady Eglantine, other than she raises pugs."

"I like dogs."

She was being deliberately argumentative and childish and Ches met like with like. "Pugs are nasty, smelly little beasts."

She giggled. "You only say that to discourage me. Do not forget, I know your mother has one and I have often seen you playing with it."

"Not since it was a pup." Discomfitted, he tried another topic, raising what he hoped to prove a more valid objection than even pug dogs combined with a dangerous sixth earl. "I have heard tell that Spadefield House is haunted!"

"No! Truly?"

Now he had her interest. She stared at him, wide-eyed, and he pursued his advantage. "It is said that the first Earl of Spadefield walks the halls when there is a full moon."

She clasped her hands in delight. Ches began to feel uncertain. This did not proceed at all as he planned. The aggravating miss bounced on her toes in excitement.

"I vow I wish to see this spectre for myself!"

Chesney opened his mouth and shut it again before he finally spoke. "Isabella, you should not carry on in this nonsensical fashion. Most likely you would faint dead away or succumb to a fit of the vapours were you to actually meet with a wraith."

"I have never done so missish a thing in my life!" she exclaimed, indignant. "I assure you, I look forward with pleasure to meeting—at least seeing—this spectre, purely in the interest of determining the truth or falsity of the rumours of its existence."

Feeling defeated, Ches prepared to take his leave. He never should have brought up the spectre of Spadefield; now the contrary girl was more than ever determined to go. But she could not brave the rigours of a house haunted by both a ghost and one he believed to be a thoroughly loose fish. Someone sane, with her best interests at heart, should keep an eye on her. Almost without realizing what he intended to do, he resolved to set up digs in Town where *his* would be the eye kept on the wilful chit, and it would be kept as well on Dysart, sixth Earl of Spadefield.

"As it happens," he said, far too casually, "I, too, shall be spending some time in London. Just as well. Someone familiar with the members of the ton should squire you about, if only to fend off gazetted fortune-hunters. It is high time you married before you do something idiotic and quite ruin yourself. Now, I have decided the qualifications essential in a husband for you—"

"*You* have decided! Chesney Carlyle, what gives you the right to choose a man for me? Do you think I cannot make up my own mind? I will have you know *I've* already decided exactly what I want!"

Taken aback, Ches shoved away the folded sheet of paper he had removed from his pocket. The girl didn't know what was best for her! Here he was offering the advice she sorely needed, and would she take it? No! It was up to him, then, to see she came to no grief.

Bella's eyes narrowed, becoming speculative as she watched his face. Surely she detected a hint of possessiveness in his manner. Or could it even be jealousy that prompted his derogation of the unknown earl? Then he was *not* indifferent to her! It was a matter of honour, after all, that kept him silent.

Isabella smiled quietly at Ches's stiff back as he took his leave. Yes, going to London might be just the thing. Had he not told her so himself?

It was hopeless to compete against Chesney's code of honour, but once in Spadefield House, perhaps she could contrive to turn it to her advantage.

Mr. Chesney Carlyle, above all, was a man with a strong sense of responsibility... and her titular host was a genuine rake....

## CHAPTER TWO

IT WAS NOT ONE of the sixth Earl of Spadefield's better mornings. He staggered from his bedchamber at noon, somewhat bleary-eyed and supporting his aching head with both hands. The dining parlour with its row of revivifying decanters on the sideboard was one flight down. Fortunately, he had no need to release one hand to cling to the bannister for guidance; his feet fitted into worn hollows in the ancient treads.

He had taken but one step when sounds from the Great Hall below betokened an arrival. The aunts were not at home. Even in his befuddled state, Dysart remembered it was Thursday, the morning the Ladies Almeria and Eglantine met at the home of a friend to maudle their innards with cat-lap and their minds with scandal-broth. It was up to him to play host. Drawing a steadying breath, he continued down.

Creswell, his butler and general factotum, waited at the foot of the stairs. "In the drawing-room, my lord." He gave a disdainful sniff. "It's him again."

"Oh, the devil. Thank you, Creswell. Lock up the silver if we have any left."

Through the open doorway, he saw a crouching figure crawling along the bottom of the wainscotting of one of the drawing-room walls, tapping, prying and twisting at protrusions. Dysart was in no mood to suffer presumption, and his brows snapped together in a thundercloud frown.

"Searching for rat holes, coz?" His patrician lip curled. "I assure you, my walls contain many."

Eustace Thorpington leapt to his feet, striking his head on the corner of a table loaded with gimcracks and upsetting it.

Dysart winced, but ever the gentleman, he refrained from comment and bent instead to raise the table and rescue his aunts' treasures. "Or were you perhaps," he continued silkily, "trying to locate the secret panel behind which old Parsifal has cached our wealth?"

Thorpington flushed and straightened his regrettably flowered waistcoat, regaining a semblance of dignity. A distant cousin, and incidentally Dysart's heir, he betrayed no family resemblance. Older and half a head shorter, he lacked the current earl's natural elegance. Always one to attempt the guise of a Bond Street Beau without the figure to support the image, he now sported the latest fashionable foible, side whiskers, an unfortunate choice. As were his next words.

"I believe I have every right to examine my future property."

For a moment, sheer murder glinted in Dysart's eyes, and Thorpington took an involuntary step backwards. The earl spoke quietly, almost in a whisper.

"If I were you, I wouldn't count on the family homestead. Spadefield House is being sold for debt. I cannot afford even to repair the roof or clean out the drains. All you may inherit from me will be a stack of arrears." He caught the flicker that crossed the other man's features. "Ah, yes. The title, of course. You want that, don't you? And you can afford to keep it in a style to which it has never been accustomed. Too bad you will not have Parsifal's mansion, as well."

"Oh, I'll have it." Thorpington's sneering tone equalled the earl's. "The sale, you know. I do not intend to await your demise. I shall be the purchaser."

Dysart's breeding stood by him. He arranged his features into gentle query while his stomach clenched in despair. Raising his eyebrows, he managed a sceptical smile. "Are you not forgetting something? Our Old Gentleman will have something to say about a usurper in his house."

"As for that," Thorpington blustered, "I'll do my searching by daylight. And perchance, bell, book and candle will take care of our ghost in short order."

Dysart shook his head. "He'll not take kindly to any attempt to evict him after two hundred years in residence. I suggest you consider such a notion with care." He looked his distant cousin up and down thoughtfully. "And perhaps not make such statements aloud within his walls."

Thorpington's pasty face paled even more, but whether from Dysart's reference to Parsifal or the ugly glint in the sixth earl's eyes, it was hard to tell. Hurriedly, the man retrieved his high-crowned beaver from the settee where Creswell had contemptuously dropped it.

Dysart's eyebrows rose again. "Leaving so soon?"

Thorpington had already reached the hall. "A pressing engagement," he called back.

The earl smiled, a cold, thin smile. "I trust it will not be with the Old Gentleman." But Thorpington was gone. Dysart's smile faded, replaced by a frown that was rapidly becoming permanent. Eustace Thorpington might indeed become the master of Spadefield House. He had the blunt to buy and there was no way the Westphale family could keep their ancestral pile off the block.

He turned towards the dining parlour, where the row of half-full decanters adorned his sideboard.

SHORTLY AFTER DYSART took himself off in search of cheering entertainment in one of the clubs, an old-fashioned crested carriage creaked and rattled up to the house. Creswell hurried down the shallow steps to open its door for the Westphale ladies. Lady Almeria accepted his offer of an elbow to lean on as she descended. Lady Eglantine clambered out on her own, drawing herself up to her full four feet ten inches and twitching her crumpled skirts into place. Almeria topped her by three inches. They weighed the same, but there the resemblance ended.

Lady Eg turned and lifted two pug dogs out of the carriage. Terpsichore, grey of muzzle and bulging of torso, waddled up the steps to the entrance on short little legs, bowed with age. Her youthful daughter, Melisande, circled her at a high-stepping prance, ignoring the querulous yaps of her crochety dam. Lady Eg shooed them before her, beaming fondly.

Once inside, the two ladies collapsed in their favourite chairs in the bookroom, Almeria with a sherry, Eg with a stiff brandy. Melisande considered leaping onto Lady Almeria's bony knees and thought better of it, disposing herself instead on the hearth rug where she remembered leaving a bone the evening before. No longer able to make the leap to a chair, Terpsichore pawed at the ankles of first one lady, then the other. Kindly Lady Eg scooped up the elderly dog and cuddled her on what lap remained of her capacious form, continuing an interrupted conversation.

"You must know, Almeria, Terpsi is quite past it. We must depend on Mel, but I am at a loss as to where I may find a worthy sire. Before, I have always used Lady Raine's Pride of Beaufort, but he has passed on to whatever great reward lies ahead for pugs of excellent conformation. Besides, he was Mel's own father."

Hearing her name, Melisande wuffled and returned to gnawing her bone, snuffling through the squashed nose that gave her the aspect of a pigmy bulldog. "Good girl," Eg assured her, then gave Terpsichore an extra pat to even the attention.

Lady Almeria sipped her sherry, frowning. "Really, Eg, I think you should wait until we at least know we have a home for her to litter in."

Eg looked up, puzzled. "Why, we shall come about. Dysart said so."

"I pray he may be right."

Somewhere prayers are answered, for at this point Creswell entered, bringing the post which had just arrived. Among the bills was a missive sealed with wax and bearing the frank of Viscount Robisham. Lady Almeria dropped the bills to the floor and broke the wax on this far more promising letter.

A few minutes passed while a gamut of conflicting emotions raced across her aristocratic features. "Good God!" she said at last.

Lady Eg looked up from tickling the tummy of the pug who lay upside down in the crook of her arm. "What?" she asked, dismayed. "Are we evicted?"

"No, no. Quite the opposite! This is from Robisham, offering to pay all the expenses of a London Season for my goddaughter, along with a substantial bonus if I will bring out the girl and find her a suitable husband."

"A come-out!" Lady Eg stared at her, aghast. "We cannot!" Her horror was understandable for Spadefield House operated of necessity with a skeleton crew of domestics. Creswell was aided by one aging footman; belowstairs, his wife reigned supreme as housekeeper—she also served as cook—and directed the duties of only one scullery maid, a laundry maid and two housemaids. Dysart had a valet, of course, but the aunts shared a lady's maid. In the mews, John Coachman had only one stable boy to help maintain the old carriage, their two horses, Dysart's curricle and his expensive pair of greys. "We cannot!" she repeated.

"Do but listen, Eg! Robisham writes that Lady Isabella brings her woman and two footmen, whose salaries he pays—"

"But we must feed and house them! There are bedchambers aplenty. Far too many, but—"

"And he encloses a letter of credit to his bank to cover their maintenance and any household expenditures we may incur. All bills for clothing, the putting on of balls, her court presentation and so on are to be directed to him."

"That letter must go to his bank at once, Almeria! Only think if he should change his mind. Creswell!" Lady Eg shouted, for the bell-pulls were out of order. Dumping the indignant Terpsichore onto the floor, she struggled to her feet. "John Coachman must bring the carriage back at once!"

In minutes, Spadefield House was thrown into uproar by Lady Almeria, who called in the housekeeper with orders to set the housemaids to scrubbing from attic to basement.

"You must hire two more immediately. And we must have a true cook, not that you are less than excellent, my dear Mrs. Creswell, but you must be free to assume your regular regime as housekeeper and manage all. We must have another laundry maid—perhaps two—and an assistant for the new cook or she will not stay. Woman, do not stand there blinking at me! We are in the funds for a time and we must take advantage of it. Go, go, for Lady Isabella will arrive any time this week. Oh, dear, there will not be time to replace the drawing-room draperies or refurbish the chairs—"

Having sent her minions flying distractedly about their business, Lady Almeria settled down to reread the precious letter while they awaited the carriage.

"Believe me, Eg," she said, "the profits from this undertaking will be a tidy sum, for mantua makers, milliners and caterers are known to be grateful for the business. Why, when Lady Bascombe brought out her cousin's niece last year, she made two hundred pounds on one presentation gown alone, and Robisham can afford to do both his daughter and us proud!"

Lady Eg was less transported. "Two hundred pounds will not go far towards reducing our mountain of debt."

"Two hundred pounds!" Almeria would have sneered like Dysart, had she not remembered her breeding. "Pence and farthings! My dearest Eg, we are saved!"

Eg looked at her anxiously, as though expecting to visit her in the future at Bedlam. "Whatever do you mean?"

"Lady Isabella must be possessed of a magnificent dowry, and she is the only child of a viscount wealthy beyond our wildest dreams."

"Yes?"

"Think! Dysart is unmarried and an earl. When Robisham says to find her a suitable husband, he can only mean for her to become Countess of Spadefield."

Lady Eg's hands flew to her mouth. "Dysart?"

"Can you doubt it? Is Robisham not sending her to us? Dysart said we should come about and, oh, indeed we shall."

Lady Eg was troubled. "But must we sacrifice Dysart?"

"Sacrifice!" Almeria gaped at her, though in a ladylike fashion. "Sacrifice? To wed *my* goddaughter?"

Lady Eg put forth a problem. "But does Robisham know Dysart? The dear boy has sometimes committed a few excesses."

Both ladies paused to consider. The viscount could know nothing of Dysart's reputation or he would not have thought for a moment of placing his daughter under the Spadefield roof.

"We should give thanks fasting for a country man's blissful ignorance," remarked Eg, at last.

"Nonsense," Almeria said briskly. "Dysart has been a trifle spoiled, I grant you, owing to being raised by two doting aunts, but there is nothing wrong with him that settling down to marriage and setting up his nursery will not cure."

"And having a fortune," Eg added, but not hopefully. She thought of another problem and her eyes widened with anxiety. "Almeria, how can we put on balls here? What of the Old Gentleman?"

Lady Almeria hesitated only a moment. "We are saving his home. He will understand. And, of course, we shall undertake no engagements when there is a full moon."

Her sister still muttered to herself, unconvinced. "Maybe we should not hold any balls at all, not even a come-out. Suppose she attracts another suitor—Dysart will lose out and we shall have had all this bother for nothing."

Almeria had sharp ears. "Don't be ridiculous. Of course Lady Isabella must have a come-out. As for other men, it will only serve to fix Dysart's interest if he sees another pursuing her."

Eg's lower lip protruded stubbornly. "He may not like her. I'll not have him wed to a female he cannot bear."

"Eglantine Westphale, must you constantly quibble so?" Her nerves already on edge, Lady Almeria came close to losing her temper. "I remember her as a delightful child."

"Suppose she does not form a tendre for him?"

"Not—that is the outside of enough! You are becoming nonsensical. How could any female resist so charming and handsome a man?"

Indeed, neither lady could imagine such a possibility. Their future seemed assured. It needed only to see Robisham's letter of credit safely to his bank, and the carriage was already at the door.

IT WAS THE DINNER HOUR before the chief player in their scheme to acquire Lady Isabella Greenlea's substantial dowry put in his appearance. Dysart could always be counted on to turn up for the main meal. The St. James's Street clubs he frequented were inordinately expensive; it was far cheaper to dine at home.

Terpsichore and Melisande met him in the hall with a chorus of delighted yaps. Stooping, he scratched them on that exact aggravatingly itchy spot at the base of a chubby pug's spine on which no amount of scrabbling and stretching could bring teeth or claw to bear. Leaving them rolling on the floor in ecstasy, he headed for the bookroom and the only lighted hearth. He paused in the doorway, and his devil-may-care expression gentled as he nodded to the aunts.

Maiden ladies were known to have an excessively soft spot in their hearts for a charming rake, and the Westphale twins were no exception. They gazed at him worshipfully, and chirped happily.

"Hallo, loves," he greeted them, planting a light kiss on each proffered cheek. "What's toward? I've never seen old Creswell so nippy on his pins." He stopped suddenly, his face a picture of dismay. "Do not tell me we have sold the house!"

"No, no. Far from it, Dysart," began Lady Almeria. "The most wondrous thing—" Then she, too, stopped, nonplussed. How to broach the subject she and Lady Eg had dissected to the finest details all afternoon? She could readily imagine the reaction of her confirmed bachelor nephew to the news of coming nuptials. She could not say the fatal words.

Lady Eg had no such reservation. "We've found you a bride," she announced, unconscious of firing a bombshell. "One who is wealthy enough to pay all our debts and save Spadefield House!"

The dogs had followed him in, and Dysart had just picked up Melisande. He dropped her on top of Terpsichore, who complained loudly. Tut-tutting, his younger aunt fussed over the insulted pugs, unmindful of her stunned nephew.

He turned to Lady Almeria, as the sanest person present. "What...what did she say?" he demanded. "I cannot have heard aright."

Almeria silently handed him the now dog-eared letter from Viscount Robisham, and waited until he had perused it.

He looked up, frowning. "But what has this to do with me?"

"We have every reason to believe," Lady Almeria explained carefully, "that Lady Isabella's father expects her to become the next Countess of Spadefield."

"You're bamming me!" He threw the missive on the floor.

Lady Eg abandoned comforting the pugs and rescued the precious piece of paper. "Only think of the amount of her dowry!" she exclaimed. "We cannot whistle such a fortune down the wind!"

He looked from one aunt to the other. "You seem to have taken the oddest notion into your heads. It's midsummer moon with you both! She would not have me."

"That will be no trouble at all," soothed Lady Almeria. "Only be your own charming self and she will not be able to resist you."

"But... but... I've no desire to be buckled for life—if she has reached the age of—of near as naught nineteen, she must be a regular antidote!"

"You do not know that. You may discover she is perfectly delightful."

"Bran-faced... fat... squinty eyed—"

Lady Eg interrupted. "But rich, Dysart."

"Bacon-brained... fubsy-faced... hen-witted—"

"Dysart!" Lady Almeria spoke sharply. "You speak of my goddaughter."

"On the shelf! Almost twenty years of age!"

Almeria had had enough. "Pray cease flying into a pucker, my dear boy. Face the truth. You must marry someday, for if you do not have an heir, Eustace Thorpington will be the next Earl of Spadefield. And you must recoup our fortune if we are to survive."

Dysart stared at her, revolted. "I am to wed her for her money? A dashed smoky thing to do! I should be labelled a gazetted fortune-hunter which, I promise you, I would not relish. So far, no one can throw *that* in my face, and I wish to keep it that way."

"No one would dare! You forget you are an earl and a very personable gentleman of excellent lineage. It will not be in the least wonderful if she does not conceive a lasting passion for you at first sight."

"Not being one puffed up in my own conceit, I do not so flatter myself! I may be an earl, but she is a viscount's daughter. An earl, especially a penniless one, would be no bargain."

He struggled in vain.

"Dysart," said Lady Almeria in a tone that brooked no argument, "the monies we may reap this Season will last only the year. We must think of the future and there will never come another opportunity the like of this one. If you do not wed an heiress, we shall yet have to sell Spadefield House and eventually, when we have gone through the purchase price, we shall all starve."

"Surely you are mistaken?" put in Lady Eg, genuinely terrified. She hugged Terpsichore to her. "Oh! Do they not feed the dogs of prisoners in the Fleet Street debtors' prison?"

Lady Almeria ignored her. "Only imagine, Dysart, how... how *lovely* to be for once beforehand with the world." She added wistfully, "No duns. No unpleasantness with the tradesmen. No more turned gowns..."

Dysart looked at his aunts, and a corner of his generous mouth turned up in a rueful smile. Truly, he was acting the selfish beast. This marriage would mean a life of comfort for the dearest people in the world, the two who had most unselfishly given up their own lives to spoiling and cosseting a lost and frightened child when his parents had died in a carriage accident, leaving him alone. He owed everything to them.

The idea of becoming leg-shackled, even to a lady with a large dowry, held no appeal. He had never intended to be caught in parson's mousetrap, being quite content in his present way of life—except for one matter. He had recently formed a tendre for a dashing widow who was not quite the thing. Outwardly almost respectable, Mrs. Fanchette Montfort, the relict of a junior army officer lost in the French campaign, supported herself by holding card parties with little suppers at her home in a shabby-genteel area of Clarges Street. She had lately thrown out lures and distinct hints that she would be quite willing to relinquish her financial struggles and be kept in luxury as a mistress. Unfortunately, Dysart lacked the wherewithal for such an enterprise... but if he were the master of a not contemptible fortune... surely it would be possible to arrive at some comfortably discreet arrangement with the Widow Montfort. But every feeling must be revolted by such a want of honour! He looked again at his aunts, both eagerly awaiting his decision. It would mean so much to them. A whole new way of life. Release from worry...security... Reluctantly he agreed to woo the wealthy young lady.

It did not occur to any of them that Lady Isabella Greenlea might have other designs.

## CHAPTER THREE

SPADEFIELD HOUSE, Lady Isabella discovered, stood not in the fashionable section of Town. And it looked the veritable haunted dwelling Chesney had promised! She hugged herself in delight. Four storeys tall, the facade of the oblong, box-like building was flanked on east and west by round crenelated towers with irregular slits for windows. Had it not been daylight, bats might have circled those ominous heights. The dead and dying leaves of dendritic branches of ivy covered the walls and had crept over the window-sills. She could readily imagine an entire company of spectres roaming within and peering out at her through the ripples and bubbles in the centuries-old glass panes that were still visible.

One of many ancient estates on the outskirts of London, Spadefield House had been caught up by the burgeoning city, swallowed by progress. During the past three hundred years, its spacious grounds were sold off, parcel by parcel, until it now stood like a dilapidated scarecrow in a crowded field of newer Town houses.

Other buildings had been remodeled, but Spadefield remained a fifteenth-century anachronism, its venerable stonework and once-rosy bricks stained and blackened by the coal smoke and soot of modern London. Bella descended from her elegant carriage onto the cobbles of a street that now ran right before the door.

It was more than a trifle disappointing to be met by a perfectly normal butler of benign, even avuncular, aspect. Two unfashionably dressed ladies, quite substantial and not in the least ghostly, waited to greet her at the open front door. On either side of them, two stout tan pug dogs sat and looked at her, each with a substantial measure of pink tongue lolling below a squashed-in black nose. Suddenly shy, she stood at the foot of the steps and looked back.

The shorter, plumper lady appeared as nervous as Bella felt, but the taller, thin one came down the steps in a rush and caught her in a scented embrace.

"Our Isabella at last! Oh, but you are like your mother!" she exclaimed. "You must know, she was my dearest friend. It will be almost like having her here once more." She stepped back, holding Bella away. "But where are my manners? I am Almeria Westphale—of course you cannot remember me—you were in your cradle when last we met—and this is my sister, Eglantine. Welcome to Spadefield House."

Behind Lady Almeria, the plump little lady burst into speech and, as though at a signal, the pugs danced about, yapping excitedly.

"You must be worn out and famished," that lady shouted over the dogs. "Even the best of carriages, which I can see yours is, do jounce and jiggle one so. Welcome indeed, my dear. Come inside at once. There is a fire in the bookroom, and Mrs. Creswell has laid out refreshments. We have a new cook, and there are biscuits and three kinds of cake and sherry—" she threw an apologetic glance at her sister who, by frowning, was attempting to dampen her to silence "—that is, negus, if you prefer."

After twenty miles of indifferent roads, Bella was indeed tired and ravenously hungry, for they had not paused on the way. Lady Eglantine had endeared herself at once. On a wave of warmth, she allowed the ladies to usher her into a great, gloomy medieval hall.

The stone walls were hung with shields and ancient weaponry. Tapestries and the pennants of bygone Westphales were draped from the baluster railing of a shadowed gallery that ran on the four sides of the chamber over her head. Cold pavingstone beneath her feet chilled through her thin slippers. Across from the huge double oaken entry doors, a massive hearth, capable of roasting entire oxen, was flanked by rusting suits of armour. Twin staircases rose on each side of it, curving upwards to join together at a landing on the gallery above.

Bella was hurried across the hall towards an open door to the right of the hearth, past carved chests and heavy black oak tables bearing copper bowls, brass urns and gleaming candelabra. Through the door, she could see a cheerfully blazing coal fire on a hob-grate in a green marble chimneypiece. Over the mantel, reaching to near the twenty-foot ceiling, a larger-than-life-size painting of a rather wild-eyed gentleman in Elizabethan rig dominated the room. An odd, tingling sensation crept over Bella as she stared at it. Could this be a portrait of the spectre that walked Spadefield's halls?

Her thoughts were distracted by Lady Eglantine's words as that lady shooed her on into the room.

"Dysart will not be home until we dine, so there is plenty of time for your maid to unpack."

Bella's tingle changed to a shiver of anticipation at the mention of Lord Spadefield's name. Her first genuine rake! After Chesney's frank warnings (which of course she intended to heed) she quite looked forward to meeting the earl, at least here in the safe surroundings of her godmama's home.

"Do be seated," Lady Almeria urged, steering her towards the hearth. Two shabby sofas were drawn up before the fire, making a cosy semi-circle along with three worn chairs and a number of needleworked hassocks. A wobbly taper-legged Hepplewhite table in the centre of the arrangement held a tray loaded with the promised cakes and decanters. "Will you not have a biscuit?" Lady Almeria asked.

"Or a frosted teacake," put in Lady Eglantine, breaking one in half for the dogs as she spoke. "And there is *both* sherry and negus," she added. "Kind Mrs. Creswell."

Bella stared about the book-lined room, fascinated. Obviously, the family lived in their library. Besides shelf after shelf of literary works, here were the ladies' sewing tables, writing desks, an elderly pianoforte and baskets for the pugs.

Until she entered the bookroom, Bella had not fully understood her father's preoccupation with the Westphale family's finances. She had thought it most odd that the viscount had insisted the carriage return to Robisham Park that very day so as not to put the household to the expense of boarding for even one night the coachman, two out-riders, the extra footman and six horses. To Bella, brought up to take for granted the presence of every luxury, signs of penury abounded on all sides, from the faded draperies at the windows to the old-fashioned mahogany of the Chippendale chairs. No wonder her father told her to spare no expense in supplying Spadefield House's every need, for he would gladly pay all bills. Why, the Westphales must be nearly at a standstill!

The Elizabethan figure in the gigantic portrait seemed to be staring down at her, and for a startled second, she almost believed he nodded and threw her a wink.

Lady Almeria, having seated Bella on one of the sofas, pressed on her a plate of cakes, while Lady Eglantine, regardless of their guest's tender age, poured three full glasses of sherry.

"Indeed, my love," said Almeria, "I cannot get over your resemblance to your dear mother. You are her very image as I remember her."

"Oh, am I?" Bella tore her eyes from the portrait, for she felt the painted face had begun to grin. "I—I hope so, for it was my dream as a child to grow up to be like her. My father has a painting of her in his bedchamber, and I was wont to slip into his room and sit on the floor while imagining her likeness coming to life."

Rather like the painted gentleman above her. She wondered if he, too, would disappoint her by remaining in his frame. There she went, fantasizing. She strove to give her hostesses her complete attention. Listening, she became enchanted, as the Ladies Almeria and Eglantine reminisced about the mother she had never known, recounting anecdotes that brought her to life far more vividly than her childhood dreams.

She had absent-mindedly finished three biscuits, two frosted cakes and a second glass of sherry when suddenly a deep gong echoed through the hall. One of the pugs looked up, crumbs stuck on the end of her lolling tongue, and the other began to bark.

Lady Eglantine leapt up. "Good heavens, what was that for? It must be an hour yet before dinner!"

"Dressing," her sister reminded her, plainly embarrassed. "Do hush, Melisande," she added to the dog. "You've heard the gong before." The pug subsided, snuffling after the remains of a cake. The older dog, unconcerned, slurped in her tongue full of crumbs and waited expectantly for more. She was out of luck, for all three ladies rose as the figure of Mrs. Creswell appeared at the door, come to escort Isabella to her chambers.

Bella, disappointed in the prosaic appearance of the butler, eyed the newcomer with delight. At last she encountered a true denizen of this haunted mansion. Mrs. Creswell, conscious of her new role as doyenne of a bevy of domestics, had elected to don her best black bombazine with the stiff white neck ruff, above which her face stuck out, red from recent scrubbing and topped by a severe cap tied under her chin with black ribbons. With her hawk-like nose and sharp little eyes, she represented, for all the world, the human form of a genteel buzzard.

She dropped Isabella a decorous curtsy. "If you'll come this way, my lady, your chamber is ready."

Hoping against hope to have been assigned one of the tower rooms, Bella hurried after her, but they went up only two flights and across a corridor to what she decided was the family wing.

Mrs. Creswell talked as they went, in a most unbuzzardly fashion. "We have given you the room next to Lady Almeria," she explained. "It will be more quiet there, as the dogs sleep in with Lady Eglantine."

Bella detected only the slightest disapproval in this last comment. Indeed, the woman spoke the names of both ladies with affectionate warmth.

"My lord Dysart," she went on, "keeps somewhat odd hours, but he'll not disturb you, being at the far end of the wing in the master chambers. Here we are, my lady."

She stopped by an open door, and Bella could see her abigail, Mattie Ludd, inside, her arms full of gowns, in the act of hanging them away in a monstrous mahogany wardrobe. Bella thanked Mrs. Creswell and paused on the threshold, looking around.

The room was not over-large, but it had two long narrow windows with pale green draperies through which the setting sun cast a rosy glow across the inlaid floor with its nice piece of Oriental carpet, a sign that the old mansion had known better days. The walls, papered above the dados with fading rosebuds, were hung with delicate watercolours, no doubt the work of one of the aunts. Besides the wardrobe the chamber contained a toilette table, a washstand on a tripod foot with a painted porcelain bowl and soap box and a bedside commode. The bed itself was high, with steps to climb up by, and a tester on a wooden framework from which depended voluminous threadbare tapestry bed hangings that once had been blue. Not a single piece in the room matched, either by style, colour or choice of wood.

Mattie, talkative as ever, had hung away her burden and now stood watching her. "Something, i'n it?" she remarked, with the freedom of ten years' association. "One of the maids told me they collected the best pieces from the other bedchambers to fix up this 'n."

"It... it's lovely, and I must tell them so."

"Lucky we brought Thomas and Henry." Mattie dove into another trunk. "You should have seen them staggering up those stairs with the trunks." She emerged with another armload of gowns, scattering silver paper across the thin carpet. "Have you laid eyes on that decrepit old gadger they have for footman here? He must have come with this stone barn. It's wonderful they still have him. These folks may be Quality, but they're poor as church mice. I've laid out your new sprig muslin."

Demure sprig muslin in which to meet an infamous rake? "No, no indeed," said Bella. "Put me into the blue with the double flounce."

The abigail pursed her lips. She knew Lady Isabella well. "You mind yourself around that Lord Spadefield, my lady. Your papa won't half cut up stiff if you come running home with a broken heart and no husband. I've heard tales of the likes of this Lord Spadefield."

"No need to go into a taking, Mattie. The blue, please. I know what I am about."

Mattie cast her mistress a sidelong glance as she laid out the blue gown with the double flounce. "They're saying belowstairs as how you've come to wed their rackety earl so's they can use your blunt to put this place to rights. I'm giving notice, here and now, my lady. I'll not live in this draughty mausoleum with himself and ghosts afoot."

Bella exclaimed in mock horror. "You're not leaving me, Mattie?"

"Course not, Miss Bella," Mattie reassured her, reverting to her schoolgirl era manners. "Just dropping a word of warning in your ear as to the intents of those sweet-looking old ladies."

Bella grinned, stepping out of her travelling gown. "Thank you, Mattie, but I've already been warned. I've no intention of throwing my cap over a windmill."

"See that you don't." Mattie sounded grim as she eased the flounced blue over Bella's head. "I daresay Mr. Chesney wouldn't like it above half, neither. Here, hold still so I can hook you. Time I was getting to your hair."

Mattie, chattering while wielding hairbrush, curling tongs and pins, passed on the tales of the earl's activities she had heard from the domestics belowstairs.

"Proud of him, they are," she explained. "Carousing at parties with regular high-flyers and escorting more than one dazzling barque o'frailty about the Town. Right expensive, he is, and the aunts have scarce a feather to fly with, him being a sad drain on their purse. Not like our Mr. Chesney. Not that he hasn't his bit o' fluff, too."

Isabella, at the moment submitting to Mattie's energetic use of the brush, kept her tongue between her teeth though she was dying to demand more of Ches and this bit o' fluff.

"Already in Town, is Mr. Chesney," Mattie went on. A blush crept over her cheeks. "There was a note from his man Coggs waiting for me in the kitchen."

Good. Isabella wanted Ches here to observe her triumphs—if she had any. And she meant to have at least one. If the Westphales truly were after her fortune, the earl should play his part in her schemes with a will. That would wake up Mr. Chesney Carlyle.

Mattie gave an extra yank at her hair. "Coggs wrote that he was free this evening, and if I could meet him, he'd be by the back gate. Mr. Ches was off to see his light skirt."

The abigail cast a sidelong glance at her lady's face in the mirror, and Bella maintained a placid expression. Very well, she already knew Ches had a mistress. She was not so green that she didn't know there was a side to the life of a single gentleman, even one of honour, that no well-bred lady knew anything about—or at least, admitted to knowing. She learned quite a lot from the talkative Mattie, and what must be the equally talkative Coggs.

When she remained silent, Mattie asked anxiously, "You won't be needing me for a few hours, will you, my lady? Just the dinner hour and a bit?"

"Of course not. You may stay out as long as you wish." *And extract as much information about Mr.*

*Ches from Coggs as you can,* she added silently, *while I flirt with the infamous earl.*

Half an hour later, complete to a shade in her favourite periwinkle blue and with her guinea-gold ringlets brushed until they gleamed in the candlelight, Isabella made her entrance. It was highly effective, but somewhat wasted, for only the aunts and the pugs were in the bookroom to which Creswell directed her. Highly disappointing, for she had counted on making an early impression on the disreputable earl since he was to be the chief weapon in her arsenal for the battle to capture Chesney's elusive heart.

And what a weapon he would be if only he'd cooperate and pursue her.

A rather stiff hour transpired, the ladies on pins and needles waiting for their nephew and Isabella feeling shy in a strange household. It was the first time she had been away from Robisham Park without her father or a contingent of close relatives.

Lady Almeria had only one subject of conversation—the amazing virtuosity in all things of her nephew. Lady Eglantine, though not so eager, added her mite until Bella began to feel like a potential buyer besieged by a pair of horse-copers determined to sell a prize prad. Even the dogs outdid themselves in being sociable. Melisande, in less than ten minutes, bounded onto her lap and Terpsichore, the elderly pug, stationed at Bella's feet, submitted graciously to having her stomach rubbed intermittently.

At long last came the sounds of arrival from the hall, Creswell's gentle accents and another's answer.

"Has she, indeed? Well, here we go, then."

Both ladies fluttered to their feet, Melisande jumped from Bella's lap and Terpsichore waddled and puffed after her out the door. Scuffling noises interspersed with "Down, girls! No, not my hat. Here, Creswell, it is for you. Do try for some decorum, you silly pups—we must go in with all dignity."

In this, the sixth Earl of Spadefield failed, for it is not easy to make a stately entrance while tripping over two dogs and being dragged forward by eager aunts, each clutching an arm.

The confusion inherent in his progress across the room gave Bella an opportunity to examine her host without the solecism of an out-and-out stare. So this was a rake, supposed to be so dangerous! The warmth between the earl and his aunts surprised her. The man could not be all bad. Raised by a well-meaning but cold-mannered father and a series of nursemaids and governesses, she had never known a loving household.

She studied the earl with a speculative eye. He was tall, cutting a rather dandified figure with stylishly tousled fair curls, undeniably a handsome man in spite of his rakish air. Especially now, when laughter softened his features as he tried to loosen the aunts' hold on his arms, managing the while to kiss each of them on the cheek and not step on one of the precious pugs. Yes, indeed, he would do to a pin. If Chesney Carlyle did not drown in a sea of green jealousy at the sight of Lord Spadefield, she was much mistaken. Therefore, she prepared to meet him with her most beguiling smile, batting her lashes like a demure country miss.

The earl managed to shake himself free of his four attendants and bowed before her with the proper grace befitting a Peer of the Realm. Taking her hand, he let his lips linger on her fingertips while he raised his eyes slowly, appraising her in a way that made her cheeks grow warm.

"Upon my word," he murmured on a wine-scented breath. "This is a pleasant surprise."

Bella realized her error. The man *was* dangerous! The devil-may-care glint in his eyes, the unseemly warmth of his manner, the caressing tone of his voice—all were calculated to send a maiden's pulse pounding. Oh, but she must take care! She scarcely heard Lady Almeria's flowery introductions. Then Mattie's words came back to her—this man wooed her fortune, not her, and she'd best remember it.

She stiffened her spine and her defences, and forced a casual acknowledgement, noting the tiny lines of dissipation about his knowing eyes and the weakness of his mouth. No, she assured herself, she was in no danger of losing her heart. Compared to the proper Mr. Chesney Carlyle, the Earl of Spadefield was a frippery rattle, not to be trusted an inch, a cozening rascal, and an unconscionable fortune-hunter, no matter how needful his cause. She tried, and did not succeed, in stifling a touch of sympathy, for according to Mattie, he and his aunts were indeed in a sorry case. But he would have to find another heiress, her heart was already given.

Now that the master of the house had returned, Creswell clouted his dinner gong with a will, setting the dogs to yapping and the aunts to twittering. The earl offered Bella his arm. After a hesitant glance at the other ladies, she accepted it and allowed herself to be led across the front hall to the dining-parlour on the other side.

They entered yet another cavernous room. In spite of candelabra on the sideboard, the ceiling vanished overhead in eerie shadows. Above dark oak dados, the walls were hung with faded tapestries in an unsuccessful attempt to counteract the damp chill of ancient stone.

Covers for four were laid on a massive mahogany table better suited to forty, with a Staffordshire dinner service, Sheffield plate and an assortment of cutlery: pistol-gripped knives, rat-tailed spoons and three-tined forks with green-stained ivory handles.

The earl seated Bella on his right, Lady Eglantine on his left, and Lady Almeria seemingly miles away at the foot of the table, before taking his place at its head.

"Surely," Bella exclaimed, "you do not dine in this way every day! My dear Godmama, you look quite lost and alone. Do come up and join us. Sit by me."

Lady Almeria came to her feet, in some confusion, but the irrepressible earl gave a snort of laughter.

"You're right, Lady Isabella. As a rule, we all crowd up here by the fire. Creswell is overcome by the honour of your visit. My good man," he called to the butler, "set us in our usual places from this day on."

Creswell, clearly glorying in his new cadre of assistants, snapped his fingers and one of the footmen scurried to move Lady Almeria's setting.

Bella rose to make room, and turned to warm her hands at the welcome heat from the hearth. The wide chimneypiece had, at some more recent time, been filled in to accommodate a Rumford stove, and here again, a coal fire smouldered on a hob-grate. The heavy oak surround of the original fireplace bore intricate carvings of what she thought at first were runic symbols. She now perceived words and bent closer, attempting to decipher them.

"Don't bother." The earl grinned. "I can quote it for you." Lowering his voice to a sepulchral chant, he began:

St. Francis and St. Benedight
Bless this house from wicked wight,
Keep it from all evil spirits,

Spectres, wraiths, and shrouded ghouls,
From curfew time to morning light.

He returned to his normal, bantering tone. "Placed there in 1651, shortly after old Parsifal went on one of his early strolls through our halls. As you see, my ancestors took every precaution."

"Really, Dysart." Lady Almeria cast Bella an uncomfortable glance. "There is no need—"

"Oh, but there is!" Bella exclaimed. "Because of your ghost. I quite look forward to being granted a sighting!"

The earl's eyebrows rose quizzically. "Are you not horrified to find yourself in a haunted house?"

"No, no. You see, Chesney—that is, a friend warned me."

"And yet you came? You are a very intrepid young lady."

Bella considered this. "I suppose I must be. I have never before had a chance to find out, for I've lived a very sheltered life. But I see no reason to fear something that can only be seen or heard and cannot physically touch one. Why, I imagine a ghostly hand would pass through me like a puff of cold breeze."

"There," said Lady Eglantine, triumphantly. "No one with sense would fear our Old Gentleman."

Lady Almeria nodded. "It is merely sheer cowardice, a lack of backbone, that leaves victims of spectral sightings white haired and senseless."

"They roll themselves up," agreed Lady Eg. "The Westphales have spent their lives within these walls for centuries and none have been harmed. Our Old Gentleman tends to his business and we tend to ours."

The sixth earl felt it time to put in a tantalizing suggestion. "We share his home in harmony, but of course we are his family. He has been known to terrify visitors."

Bella turned to him eagerly. "Has he truly been seen?"

"Not by me, I'm sorry to say. Though tales abound from my grandfather's time." He must have noticed the disappointment on her face, for he hastened to add, "But we have heard him. He walks for the full moon. His footfalls echo along the corridors of the upper floors and down the stairs, accompanied by an odd thumping or clanking sound."

"Dragging something," Bella breathed, enthralled. "But why does he walk? What holds him to this house?"

"Our entire fortune," said Lady Eg.

Lady Almeria was more expansive. "A king's ransom in family jewels, or in his case, a queen's. Parsifal was the first Earl of Spadefield, and he made the error of supporting Princess Elizabeth in the rebellion against Mary I in 1554. He was forced to go into hiding, taking with him the entire treasure of Spadefield for safe keeping. Four years later, when Elizabeth became Queen, Parsifal failed to resurface. He had vanished, and so had our fortune. Since then, his descendants have survived by their wits."

"A commodity," the sixth earl remarked, "which the male members have been sadly lacking."

"Dysart!" cried Lady Eg. "How can you say so when it is you who has kept the roof over our heads with your clever gaming."

He gave her a wry grin. "My point, exactly."

Bella broke in. "But has no one searched for this treasure?"

"Oh, yes," Lady Almeria assured her, nodding. "Five generations of Westphales have combed Spadefield House from attics to cellars. There is no treasure here."

Dysart grinned. "It's my guess the Old Gentleman absconded to the Continent with every valuable trinket he could lay hands on and no doubt lost every farthing at the gaming tables. He was, after all, a Westphale."

Isabella refused to accept this theory. "Why, if he carried away his hoard, would he still walk these halls? I believe he is here, guarding his treasure."

"No such luck, I'm afraid. Sorry," Dysart commiserated. "I, too, once believed. Now I am certain it is only his burden of guilt that keeps him earthbound."

Creswell entered, followed by the footmen bearing the first course, and the topic was dropped, but Bella had not given up. She *liked* the two ladies and even the earl had his charming moments. These people *needed* that fortune, and she meant to search for it. She was sure only a genuine hidden treasure would keep the responsible spirit bound to safeguard the secret for centuries.

If Parsifal should appear, he might guide her to his cache. She shivered with delight. What an adventure she was having! And she had expected a London Season, meant only to capture the heart of Chesney Carlyle, to be nothing but a frivolous round of social events!

That night, alone in the dark in a strange bedchamber, she lay awake for almost an hour but nothing untoward occurred. The moon, she decided, was not yet at the full. Then, just as she drifted off to sleep, she was startled by a series of hideous moans and groans. Could it be the ghost? She slipped hopefully from her room and traced down the sounds, only to discover one of Lady Eglantine's pugs, the elderly Terpsichore, was prone to snoring.

A disappointment, but she was not one to give up. Maybe tomorrow night...

# CHAPTER FOUR

THE AUNTS WERE ALREADY at table when Creswell showed Bella into the smaller breakfast room behind the formal dining parlour. Here she met a more cheerful aspect, this room having been panelled at some recent period in a lighter wood and papered between the dados and frieze in faux green marbling. Etched glass French doors opened, in more pleasant weather, onto a tiny terrace and bordering shrubbery.

Her entry caused an instant flurry, Lady Almeria directing her to a chair next to the head of the cherry-wood table and Lady Eglantine hurrying off to the billiard room on the far side of the Great Hall. Bella suspected she had gone to fetch the earl, no doubt adjured to wait there for her arrival.

Thanks to Mattie's warning, Bella knew well in which quarter blew the wind, and she observed their machinations with amusement. She wished them good fortune—but not hers. Far better to locate Parsifal's hoard.

The sixth Earl of Spadefield, like a dramatic actor, stopped just inside the door, surveying the company assembled on stage. Bella felt again a pleasurable prickling of excitement, that quickening awareness every woman knows in the presence of a dangerous male. *Take care!* her common sense admonished. *Remember, his designs are on your wealth, not your pretty figure.*

He came towards her at once, Terpsichore waddling behind, and Melisande weaving between his feet. Somehow, he reached her side without falling over the pug, and Bella noticed his reddened eyes and the pallor of his freshly shaven cheeks, due no doubt to lack of sleep. It would not have been wonderful if he had gone on a round of the clubs after she and the aunts retired. His charming manners, however, were unimpaired. He bowed over her hand as though she were a princess.

"And I thought," he said, his eyes as caressing as his tone, "only the sun could so brighten a room."

She smiled, and kept her own voice light and airy. "Good morning, Lord Spadefield. I had not expected to see you about so early."

"Did you not?" He shook his head. "With the promise of such beauty awaiting?" He gestured gallantly at the chafing dishes on the sideboard, where Creswell stood frozen like an elegant statue. "May I not fill a plate for you?" he offered.

The dogs had taken up their places, one on each side of Lady Eglantine's chair, and she was loading saucers for them, slices of ham, buttered eggs and jelly spread on muffins. The selection looked delicious, and Bella requested the same.

A maid, not a footman, carried in a fresh plate of eggs, and Lady Almeria raised her eyebrows at the butler.

"Edward, the new footman, has left us, my lady," he explained.

"Why?"

Creswell coughed and cleared his throat, glancing at Isabella. He apparently decided it would be of no use to dissemble. "It seems, my lady, he had reason to come down to my pantry in the night and he claims to have seen the Old Gentleman on the stairs."

"Nonsense," said Lady Almeria. "The moon is not at the full. And what would Parsifal be doing downstairs?"

"Why," Dysart told her, "the silver in the pantry, of course. No wonder we are left with nothing but plate."

"Dysart, do not be ridiculous. The man could not have seen him. He has not appeared to anyone in years."

Lady Eg swallowed a chunk of muffin. "If Edward has been sneaking down to Creswell's pantry, he was no doubt in his cups and filled with tales by the other servants. No wonder he fancied he saw our ghost."

Bella kept silent but she shivered with anticipation. Whether the footman actually saw the Old Gentleman was of no moment. It was three weeks only until a full moon, and then, the first Earl of Spadefield would not fail her.

Soon after breakfast, Dysart took his leave and the ladies retired to the cosy bookroom to discuss Bella's coming Season.

"For there is a problem," Lady Almeria told Bella. "We have had a late start."

"Everyone will be ahead of us," explained Lady Eg. "All the best evenings will be bespoken."

Almeria waved her calendar. "We must fill in where we can. There will be no difficulty with your Court Presentation, but as to the first really open evening for your come-out ball, it will be almost a fortnight after your formal bow before we could be assured of adequate guests."

Creswell cleared his throat gently at the door.

"A Mr. Chesney Carlyle, my lady. Are you at home?" he intoned, at his most formal.

"Ches!" Bella exclaimed, bouncing to her feet. "How lovely. Do show him in." She paused, mortified. "Oh, dear, I should not have done that. For a moment, I quite forgot I was not at Robisham Park. Pray forgive me, dearest Godmama!"

"For feeling at home? Nonsense, my precious child. Nothing could make me happier. I collect this gentleman is an acquaintance?"

"Yes, indeed. Our nearest neighbour."

Lady Almeria inclined her head towards the waiting Creswell. "Certainly we are at home. Mr.—Carlyle, is it?—cannot fail to have heard our voices."

Creswell retired. In another moment, Ches's tall figure appeared in the doorway to the hall, and Bella knew a quickness of breath, a beating of her pulse and the tingle of a very different awareness than that occasioned by the presence of Lord Spadefield. One glance at Ches, and the charms of the sixth earl were as water under a bridge.

She'd always considered Ches superlatively handsome in his country tweeds and buckskins; in his London turnout she thought him magnificent, rivalling the subdued elegance of Beau Brummel. How could she have forgotten in less than a week, how infinitely more handsome than any other gentleman was her beloved Ches? Indeed, his romantically classic features cast even Lord Byron in the shade—his shoulders broader, his dark hair curlier, his eyes the blue of a summer sky, his smile... Her heart skipped faster as he saw her and his face lit as though touched by Dysart's sun. The dimple-creases in his cheeks, the cleft in his determined chin, deepened as the warmth in his eyes spread to that special smile. Before she thought, she ran to him.

He caught both her hands in his strong grasp. "Hallo, Izzy. My, you're fine as fivepence in your Town rig."

Bella heard one of the aunts catch a startled breath behind her and saw consternation on both faces as she turned to make introductions. Obviously, they had expected an older man, a friend of her father's.

But that was just what Chesney was. Some instinct told her she'd best stress that acquaintance. She led Ches forward.

"May I make known to you Mr. Chesney Carlyle, the son of Sir Arthur Carlyle, and a close friend of my father's. I collect he has been enjoined to make certain of my safe arrival."

His special smile now included both ladies. "Indeed, Robisham would never forgive me if I did not call to ascertain that all is well with Lady Isabella."

The aunts twittered their replies to his formal greetings, which were accompanied by two of his most elegant bows. Never had Bella seen Ches so on his dignity. Her heart swelled with pride, and she surreptitiously watched both ladies as Ches, having been adjured to sit on the sofa, made polite conversation about the attractions of London he thought Bella might enjoy. Both the sisters seemed to relax, falling under the spell of his grave and decorous manner.

She was a bit surprised to learn that Ches could charm the females as easily as the Earl of Spadefield, though in an entirely different way.

Even the dogs were ecstatic over him. Melisande jumped into his lap, leaving paw prints on his pristine inexpressibles, while the elderly and arthritic Terpischore contented herself with chewing on the tassels of his Hessians. Showing a countryman's ease, he coped with a gentle "Down, madam," and a firm "None of that, my girl." He was making an excellent first impression, to her delight, for she intended to see a great deal of Mr. Chesney Carlyle.

Ches remained only the socially correct half-hour, but they had a few minutes alone in the gloomy Great Hall when she walked with him to the door. He put his hands on her shoulders and turned her to face him. Bella looked up at the handsome head bent towards her, conscious of the warm pressure, the solidity of his body so close to hers, and she knew a wild desire to throw her arms about his neck again and be kissed. For a moment, his hands slid down as though he were about to take her into a lover's embrace, but they merely stopped at her elbows, giving her a slight shake before he let her go.

"Is everything well with you here, Izzy?" he asked. "Are you content to stay?"

She managed to match his friendly tone. "Oh, yes, and no spectral manifestations in the halls at night, I'm sorry to say."

He grinned. "I'm glad of that." He fished in his pocket and produced a card on which he scribbled a few lines with one of the new graphite pencils. "Here, Bella. My directions in case you have need of me."

"I shall have every need," she said earnestly. "Of that you may be sure."

"Oh, I am. It will be my pleasure to escort you about at first until you have made some acquaintance. It's as well I shall be staying in Town for some time, for you will need someone who is up to snuff to warn off libertines—and gazetted fortune-hunters." With one finger, he lightly touched the tip of her nose. "See that you behave yourself."

Bella leaned against the door after it closed behind him, more resolute than ever to somehow capture his elusive heart. Meeting the Earl of Spadefield had made her realize as never before how deeply in love with Chesney Carlyle she had become. Nowhere could she ever find his equal. But she also realized, as she hadn't before, that he still considered her a child, to be taken care of and guided, not kissed in shadowy halls. That was about to change, if she had anything to say about it. Oh, why could not the dangerous Dysart have remained at home this morning so she could have begun her campaign by flirting with him in front of Ches? Truly, it was most inconsiderate in him.

Lady Eg, who had a penetrating voice, was speaking as Bella headed back across the hall to the bookroom.

"I for one am not in the least worried," she was saying. "He is not a dandy nor is he as dashing as our darling. And how could any maiden not prefer an earl to a mere mister?"

*Easily!* Bella thought. She purposefully bumped a table and rattled a bowl against an urn before entering the library. Both aunts eyed her anxiously as she came in.

"Is Mr. Carlyle a *very* old friend?" Lady Almeria asked.

Ah, then they definitely saw him as a rival to their beloved Dysart. Had Ches somehow betrayed a particular interest in her? If he had—oh, he must have done to make the aunts so uneasy! She hugged the thought inside herself, and schooled her tone to one of nonchalant surprise.

"Mr. Carlyle? Chesney? Why, we grew up together. I've known him all my life." She perceived signs of distress on both their faces and quickly added, "He is like an older brother to me," for she had no intention of discouraging their efforts to encourage their nephew to court her. She *needed* Dysart. Had Ches never seen the charming earl, she wondered; had they ever met?

They had, and were about to do so again.

CHESNEY LEFT Spadefield House feeling slightly relieved. He approved heartily of Lady Almeria and Lady Eglantine. Isabella, he felt, was in good hands if only she could be counted on to keep her distance from the rakish earl.

He had received a shock upon seeing young Bella in one of the extremely becoming gowns ordered by her father for her appearance in the Metropolis. She had grown to be a beauty, but that had never caused him concern while she remained in the country under the wing of the viscount. Anxiety surged through him as he realized he had no control over the chit. He might warn off undesirable males, but he could not order her actions. She was no missish maiden, but a green girl. Trouble loomed ahead, and not only from the penniless earl. Good God, every skirter in Town would be dancing attendance on her and attempting to fix her interest! It was devilish fortunate he'd been long-headed enough to come to Town where he could keep his eye on her.

The Earl of Spadefield also rated close inspection. Chesney knew the man slightly, and knew a great deal more of him from hearsay. Enough so, his uneasy feelings grew. The only way to prove or disprove the rumours would be to see for himself. Pausing at his lodgings off St. James's Street only long enough to send a message of regret to the unlucky host expecting him that evening—and to change his dog-damaged breeches—he went in search of the sixth earl through London's gentlemen's clubs.

He ran him to earth in Brooks's, a long, gloomy hole and not one of his favourites. In a room where the average man stood five feet four, the earl's six-foot frame was easy to spot. The devil was in it that Spadefield cut a handsome figure, well set up and personable of features. He could easily see an impressionable female losing her heart to such a man. He was sorely tempted to dislike the earl on first sight, but his honourable nature forced him to reserve judgement until he had furthered their acquaintance.

For several minutes, Ches remained near the door, studying his quarry's reckless play at one of the tables. Dysart was losing heavily and drinking apace.

Ches frowned. There was about the young earl's manner the air of one who had given up hope and no longer cared. His curiosity piqued, Ches walked over as a round ended, and challenged the earl to a game of piquet for pound-points.

"I find myself in need of a partner," he explained.

With a careless gesture, Dysart threw down the dice he held. "Why not? I've no luck with the ivories."

Moving only a trifle unsteadily, he joined Ches at one of the smaller tables, near the hearth on the other side of the room. In a short time, Ches had allowed him to win back a few hundred pounds and had the satisfaction of seeing the young man's spirits rise. By the third hand, Dysart, now more than a trifle on the go, had raised Ches to the status of lifelong bosom companion and confidant.

He leaned across the table, lowering his voice to what he intended for a whisper. "Do you admire fair women?" he asked.

Chesney admitted that he did.

"I don't," said the earl, draining the dregs of his wine. He tipped the bottle Ches had ordered over his glass. "Or thin ones, either." He waggled a wavering finger in front of Ches's nose. "No names, now. Both gentlemen here. Never mention the name of a lady."

"I won't," said Ches.

"Innocent maidens," muttered the earl. "No appeal for me." He staggered to his feet. "I'm going to drown myself. In the Thames."

Ches caught his arm and eased him back into his chair. "Don't do that—you'd get dreadfully wet."

Dysart blinked at him owlishly. "Better to go as a monk?"

"Much better." Ches signalled a waiter and sent him for coffee. "Strong and black."

The earl muttered to himself as they waited for its arrival. "Damned if I'll be a gazetted fortune-hunter. Not an honourable thing to do."

With this Ches agreed heartily. "Absolutely not. You stick to that conviction."

"I can't," Dysart mourned, his face crumpling like a child's. "I have two aunts."

Ches looked at him, puzzled. This seemed a non sequitur, until suddenly it dawned on him that Bella stood in more danger than he had thought if those two ladies in Spadefield House had designs on her fortune. Ladies, he knew, had not the innate sense of honour which bound gentlemen—and they exerted an all-powerful control over their male relatives.

"A queenly woman," the earl remarked forlornly to the bottom of his glass. "Chestnut hair, eyes the golden-brown of autumn leaves." He waxed poetical. "An angel from heaven, a Helen of Troy... Cleopatra... Venus... 'She walks in beauty, like whatever-it-was in the night.' " He looked up, maudlin tears glistening in his eyes. "Everything a man could desire, and I can not have her."

Ches, his attention caught, realized he was listening to a man in the grip of a powerful infatuation. Bella, then, was safe. Or was she? He must not forget the aunts! But this affair, this passing fancy or lasting passion—whatever—on the part of the earl was a thing to be forwarded at all cost.

"How came you to meet this Incomparable?" he prodded. "Tell me more. No names, of course."

Dysart raised his head again. "Certainly not." The coffee arrived and he choked over a mouthful. "Damn," he remarked. "Hot. Met her walking in the Park." He drank more coffee and leaned back, his head clearing. "She had trouble with some bounder just as she came abreast of me. Naturally—" he hiccoughed "—naturally I came to her aid."

"Ah. A woman walking alone?" Ches shook his head.

"All *comme il faut*," the earl assured him hastily. "She is a widow. And with her beauty, she can't help attracting men."

Chesney began to have grave doubts as to the respectability of the earl's great love.

"Used to be an opera dancer," continued Dysart, putting paid to Ches's suspicions. "Before she married. Husband was a line officer, killed on the Peninsula. Forced to make her own way."

Ches nodded. "I see." And he was sure he really did see. The earl's widow obviously was not quite the thing. No wonder his aunts wished to marry him off to Bella. "I collect you plan to set her up in style."

"No such thing!" the earl exclaimed, profoundly shocked. "She's a respectable female. Besides, I haven't the blunt. The creature is expensive beyond my means. No, it is merely that she is a pleasant companion. A man enjoys the company of a charming female at dinners and card parties."

"She gives card parties?"

"In her own house on Clarges Street. Has to support herself somehow or go home by beggar's bush. That husband of hers was a caper-witted waste-thrift and quite run off his legs. Left her destitute, but she's not one to go under the hatches. She makes a fair living from her tables and serves an excellent supper."

Dysart drained his coffee cup, well on the way to becoming what to him was sober. "See here, Carlyle. Why do you not accompany me to a party at her home tonight? To take place at midnight. The witching hour, you know."

"No, really..." Ches began.

"Come along. It is to be quite out of the common way. We are to attempt a seance."

"A what?"

"A meeting for the purpose of contacting the spirit of one who's passed on."

"Balderdash," said Ches.

"No, no. It is the latest kick of fashion. All the crack. Fanny—Mrs. Montfort—is Scottish, you must know, and claims to have the 'sight.' We are in for the greatest lark! Everyone will be there. I hear even Devron is to join us."

Ches froze, suddenly alert. His Grace, the Duke of Devron? The very man for Isabella! Still young, surely not much above forty, highly respected by all and reasonably presentable. Surely he'd fill all the qualifications on his list. Yes, Devron would do well for Isabella. He'd best make the man's acquaintance and throw him in her way.

"I shall be pleased to accompany you," he informed the Earl of Spadefield.

# CHAPTER FIVE

AT HALF AN HOUR to midnight, Chesney was escorted by the sixth earl to the home of Mrs. Fanchette Montfort. It was not in the best of neighbourhoods, situated on Clarges Street, above Curzon and a bit too close to Lambeth Mews.

They were ushered into a parlour where several other gentlemen waited. The room they entered was far more ornate than the fashionable interiors Ches was accustomed to. There were too many swags about the heavy red draperies, too many pillows on the sofas and prints on the walls. Numerous pedestal tables, loaded with gimcracks, created areas of danger for the unwary. And over all, the mingled aromatics: musk, patchouli, and the oils of champac and bergamot. The potpourri of fragrances dizzied his senses.

In the centre of the room, surrounded by chairs as if ready for a banquet, stood a large round table with a single, black, unlit taper in a stand. The effect was ritualistic, even ceremonial, and Ches began to wonder what bobbery he had let himself in for. A sudden stir in the room caught his attention.

The Widow Montfort made her entrance, and in that startled moment, a certain raven-haired opera dancer faded from Ches's memory. A host of unexpected thoughts flitted through his usually chivalrous mind. What an opulent armful Mrs. Montfort would be.... It was quite within the code of a gentleman, even one of the highest honour, to discard a mistress—properly recompensed, of course—and take another... and from her manner, he discerned that this ravishing creature was ripe for the taking. He had always preferred dark-haired ladies, but now he encountered a tumble of red curls, flashing green eyes and a figure that made him look frantically in any direction but at his hostess's décolletage.

The poor woman, he hurried to remind himself, was a widow struggling for her very existence in an expensive world. She must do what she must to survive. Having himself lost a young cousin at Waterloo, he felt a rush of sympathy and an urge to come to her rescue. Ches awoke from his musings when he bent to kiss the lady's hand and met her calculating gaze. Aye, she would appreciate being rescued by one of his wealth. He perceived more than a hint of invitation in her smile, but it was nothing to the welcoming warmth she bestowed on the earl before moving on to greet the next guest.

Dysart watched her go, following her every move with a fatuous smile. "What think you now?" he asked. "Is she not an angel come to earth?"

This was not exactly what Ches was thinking, but close enough. "She is indeed, ah, impressive."

"Fan is in alt over tonight's experiment," the earl went on. "She is to go into a trance! A Gypsy who told her fortune at a fair discovered that Fan is unusually perceptive and has occult powers. Because of having the 'sight,' you know, so of course, she was bound to have a go." He wandered off while he still talked, drawn after his red-haired siren.

Ches shrugged. *Chacun à son goût*. More to his taste, refreshments appeared. A maid roamed about the room carrying a tray of glasses, and decanters had joined the gimcracks on the tiny tops of the pedestal tables, miraculously able to fit. Wine flowed freely and Ches, conscious of being in a pleasant fuzz, was quite ready to accept whatever might come.

Curiosity brought a motley assembly to Mrs. Montfort's parlour, and Ches noticed that several dropped a few folded flimsies into a bowl subtly placed on a chest near the door. Donations accepted, eh? As he started over to rectify his omission, Eustace Thorpington, with whom he had a slight acquaintance, entered the room. An old hand, no doubt, for he paused by the bowl at once and ostentatiously deposited not a pony but a monkey. The man then made straight for the widow and hovered possessively at her side, much to the obvious annoyance of the sixth earl. And to that of Chesney Carlyle. So Dysart had a rival for the—well, not affection—"company" of the widow. Ches knew a sudden urge to make an attempt to cut the other man out.

He was distracted a moment later, for hard on Thorpington's heels came the Duke of Devron, the man he wished to meet. Ches backed unobtrusively into a corner and subjected the duke to a critical survey. In his mind, he went over his list of qualifications one by one. Of Devron's rank, there was no question. Lineage? He noted the man's bulging eyes and potentially corpulent figure, suggesting a not-too-distant relationship to the Regent. His clothing met the highest standard of fashion, not as severe as Ches himself preferred, yet not that of a dandified pink of the ton. Diamonds sparkled in his neckcloth and from both hands. What else was on that list? Confound it, he'd better carry the dratted paper with him for occasions such as this. He tried to remember.

Fortune? An aura of wealth and consequence surrounded the duke, moving lesser men from his path like a physical force as he made his stately way to his hostess. His manners were impeccable. His disposition? Frankly, Ches had always considered the duke something of a bore, and while he knew little of Devron's intelligence, surely the strength of his other qualifications outweighed any minor infractions in that quarter. As for his being presentable, deep down, Ches recognized a secret comfort in the knowledge that such an unprepossessing figure created no competition for himself as the duke did in the other points on his list. His self-esteem required he not lose to a better man. Lose out he must, but only because of rank. Yes, indeed. Here was an excellent *parti* for Lady Isabella, the very sort of man he had in mind.

Dysart appeared at his side, in a very ill temper, "Rag-mannered," the earl muttered. "Regular curst rum touch. The cawker's a presumptuous skirter!"

For a startled moment, Ches had a problem in discerning the subject of Dysart's diatribe, then realized the epithets were aimed at Thorpington, not the duke.

"What is that cozening jackanapes doing here?" the furious earl demanded.

The reason for the man's presence became apparent when Mrs. Montfort called for their attention and seated them around the table with the black candle. The duke sat at his hostess's side as his inherent right, and Thorpington managed to shoulder Dysart aside in the rush to claim the other choice seat. Chesney secured a pair of chairs for them opposite the widow.

The maid snuffed the remaining candles in the room, and Mrs. Montfort lighted the single taper. "You must all hold the hands of those on either side of you," she ordered. "That's to ensure that our circle is in complete spiritual harmony. Now we must have absolute silence."

She had a pleasant voice, Ches thought, low and carrying, well suited to theatrics. He reached for

Dysart's hand and found it trembling. Good heavens, the man believed in this ridiculous farrago!

Mrs. Montfort, her face lit from below in the eerie flickering of the one candle, closed her eyes and leaned back in her chair, preparatory to going into a trance.

"One among us," she intoned, "has called us together to help him communicate with a distant ancestor who left us more than two centuries ago."

"The devil one has!" Dysart hissed in Ches's ear. "It must be Thorpington! He's after old Parsifal, damme if he's not!" He began to rise from his chair, determined to challenge his cousin on the spot.

Ches restrained him with some difficulty, pulling him back. "All flummery," he whispered. "Be quiet. Let's wait and see."

"But this is the outside of enough! He means to learn the whereabouts of our treasure!"

"If he learns it here," Ches informed him, "then so will everyone else in the room. Come, take hands again, but be assured nothing will happen."

And nothing did, though the company sat in silence for some time in the darkened room, staring at the flame of the single candle. As a seance, the widow's party seemed doomed to failure.

A largish pug wandered in and distracted Chesney's attention. It snuffled asthmatically about his Hessians, the tassels of which he'd barely rescued from mastication by Lady Eglantine's dog. With his hands held, there was no way of removing the inquisitive pug short of kicking it, and he was incapable of such an outrageous breach of etiquette. He caught himself wondering if his lack of concentration interfered with their communication with the afterlife. Good lord, he was nearly believing this idiotic gammon!

Suddenly, the dog threw back its head and howled.

"Attila!" Mrs. Montfort cried, abandoning her trance. "He is here!"

Ches straightened in his chair, admitting to an involuntary moment of anxiety. Had she actually summoned the spirit of the great Hun?

But no. "Good doggie," the widow crooned. "Come, Attila. Animals know," she told her guests triumphantly, patting the dog's head. "My precious Attila sensed a presence!"

*Yes*, thought Ches. *The presence of that confounded female pug who gnawed on my boots.*

The rest of the group, vastly encouraged, concentrated even harder, staring unblinkingly at the flickering taper. All except the sixth earl, whose feverish gaze rested on Thorpington, ready to intercept any message the first earl might deem to send. Parsifal, however, remained mute and aloof.

"I knew the Old Gentleman would never hold any traffic with that abominable cawker," Dysart whispered to Ches, with a deal of satisfaction.

No further manifestations were forthcoming and the gathering broke up, not altogether disappointed. Attila's reaction (though attributed to

Chesney's boots, which he did not explain) was generally held to be conclusive proof of Mrs. Fanchette Montfort's occult powers.

Ches grinned to himself and winked at the pug. As long as everyone was happy. A trifle above par from the numerous glasses of the widow's wine he had consumed, he felt mightily pleased his unwitting contribution had made her party a success.

Dysart appeared uncertain which direction to take when they left, so Chesney steered his wandering steps towards Spadefield House, gleaning much of the legend of the resident spectre between the lines of the earl's jeremiad on the subject of Eustace Thorpington. After he finally deposited Dysart on his own doorstep, Ches found his thoughts returning to Mrs. Montfort's multiple charms.

There was naught seriously wrong with the widow as yet. Though by no means one of the Quality, she still maintained a certain respectability, but if she continued along her present path—holding the bank at her card parties and being seen with the likes of the sixth earl—she would not only be thought to exhibit a want of propriety but would acquire a shady reputation. His intrinsic chivalrous nature, aided by the fumes of his libations, came to the fore. The poor creature was a widow, struggling to survive on the fringes of the expensive Polite World. It was not for him to constitute himself judge of his fellow man.

Or woman. There could be no mistaking Mrs. Montfort for anything but a female. And one more to be pitied than one censured by Society.

He could not help but know his own respectability and honourable reputation were considered axiomatic by the ton. Perhaps he could lend her countenance by being seen to drive her in Hyde Park.... The idea took hold. A mild flirtation with a widow, one who he was certain understood the rules of the game, would not be amiss. That it would demonstrate to a certain golden-haired chit that he had other interests was not the least of the advantages of the undertaking.

Pleased with his noble resolve to aid in preserving an unfortunate lady's reputation, he retired to his lodgings to sleep off his potations. He felt secure in the knowledge that his decision was right and honourable, for both himself and Isabella.

He was not often so wrong....

THE NEXT AFTERNOON, at the fashionable hour of five, Bella was taken by Lady Eglantine for a drive around the Park in the Spadefield barouche. On their second circuit, Lady Eg suddenly gripped her arm and pointed.

"There! See!"

And Bella saw. Ahead of them, Chesney drove his high-perch phaeton and beside him sat a red-haired beauty.

Bella gasped. "That must be his...his—" She stopped, uncertain of the term. *Flaunting that female!* she thought, furious. Right on the public carriageway under the very eyes of the cream of Polite Society! Just as Mattie Ludd described her—a head full of loose curls—and looser morals. But such a quantity of hair! Could it all be hers, Bella wondered. And the same question applied to the woman's figure.

But wait. Surely Ches's light skirt had raven hair, according to Mattie's information from the man Coggs. And the redhead Mattie's belowstairs gossip had reported to be Dysart's love. Had Mattie confused the two? Or could it be both men were infatuated with the same—she couldn't say "lady"— creature, then? Both Chesney and Dysart captivated by that...that—

A sharp pain around her upper arm cut into her thoughts. Lady Eg still clutched her with fingers that bit to the bone. However, she pointed not at the questionable female but at a sturdy pug dog seated on her lap.

"I must speak to that lady," she uttered. "At once!"

"What!" exclaimed Bella.

"The sire for Melisande's pups." Lady Eg breathed the words in a sort of rapture. "He is perfect." She raised her voice. "Coachman, catch up to that phaeton."

"No!" Bella cried. "Please do not. I fear that is no lady."

Lady Eg turned to her in consternation. "Are you sure? How can you know?"

Bella stiffened. "Did you not notice? That is Mr. Chesney Carlyle driving that phaeton. And my abigail tells me... that is... you must know..."

Lady Eg said she did know. "But if I cannot speak to one of that female's class, how am I to... that is..." Now it was she who floundered on the verge of discussing a very indelicate subject. Not being one to tread lightly, she barged ahead. "How am I to arrange a meeting with that outstanding dog when Melisande's time is ripe?"

She need not have been concerned for Bella's innocence. The girl scarcely heard, her blazing eyes still fixed on Chesney's phaeton. Bella stared straight ahead, lost in dreams of scratching that lovely face and perhaps tearing out a few handfuls of that red hair.

WHILE LADY EGLANTINE and Isabella drove in the Park, Lady Almeria sat at her writing desk in the bookroom, absorbed in composing a note to Maria Sefton. She knew the generous countess, a bosom-bow of both the sisters in their girlhood, could be depended upon to help her old friends launch an eligible miss into The Marriage Mart. As one of the patronesses, Maria would gladly provide the precious voucher that would admit Isabella to that holy of holies, Almack's Assembly Rooms.

It was a godsend, Almeria thought, that she had insisted on maintaining their subscription to the rooms. Eg had complained that ten guineas a year was an exorbitant price to keep up a pretence of prosperity, but now they would reap the benefit.

A distant clanging from the butler's pantry below brought up her head. Someone had pulled the ancient bell rope at the front doors. Who could be calling at this hour of the afternoon when ordinarily both ladies would be out?

Creswell, having admitted the caller, appeared in the doorway. "Mr. Eustace Thorpington, my lady," he announced with a curling lip. "Shall I tell him you are not at home?"

Wasted, for Thorpington followed on his heels. Lady Almeria laid down her quill in irritation as the man brushed Creswell aside. She eyed her distant relative with disfavour. And with reason.

Wadding plumped the shoulders of Thorpington's bottle-green coat. The waist was nipped in to the point of discomfort, both to himself and to the straining buttons of his unfortunately flowered waistcoat. The hat he doffed as he entered her presence had a tall, conical crown and a narrow brim. His intricately tied neckcloth and the starched collar points that dented his cheeks held his head in so rigid a clamp that he could only turn it by twisting his entire upper body. He paused by the door, awaiting her approbation under the mistaken impression that his extreme costume lent him the air of a pink of the ton. She merely waited for him to approach.

After bowing carelessly over her hand, he stood back, gazing up at the immense portrait of the first Earl of Spadefield above the chimneypiece.

"I detect a distinct resemblance to myself, do not you, Lady Almeria?" he asked, an insufferably smug note in his voice. "The eyebrow there, and a certain twist to the lip."

He turned towards her as he spoke, striking the pose held by the painted earl. On the mantel behind him, the four figurines, the pair of silver candlesticks and the French porcelain clock bedecked with a shepherd, a shepherdess, three sheep and a dog began to tremble.

"The only resemblance I see," Lady Almeria returned flatly, too annoyed to notice the action on the chimneypiece, "is that you are both men." *And of you I retain considerable doubt,* she reflected to herself. "What do you want here, Eustace?"

"Why, to aid you, of course." Without being invited to do so, he seated himself in Dysart's favourite chair. "Word has reached me that you entertain a fair guest this Season. I trust the expense will be too much for you and have come to alleviate your distress."

Lady Almeria raised her aristocratic eyebrows. "Indeed?" An icicle formed on the word and dripped on the carpet between them.

The freeze failed to chill Thorpington's gloating manner. He continued smoothly. "I am come with a proposal which I am sure will meet with your favour. I understand Spadefield House is shortly to be placed on the market, and I have decided to make Dysart an offer for its immediate purchase."

Cold fury paled Lady Almeria's cheeks. This was insult added to long-standing injury. Not only did Thorpington become the next Earl of Spadefield if Dysart failed to produce a legitimate heir, but now he wished to put them out of their ancestral home. Only her breeding kept her from taking up a vase full of flowers that stood all too handy on a nearby table and striking him on his modish curly pate. The temptation to destroy his valet's hour of labour with the hot tongs grew almost too much for her. She spoke through gritted teeth. "I must thank you for your consideration for our welfare, Eustace, but I assure you it is completely unnecessary."

Her anger propelled her into an error of judgement. With ill-concealed triumph she informed him that Dysart was to marry Lady Isabella and her fortune, set up his nursery at once and cut his distant cousin out as the heir.

"We are even now meeting the worst of our creditors partway," she said. "And all have agreed to hold off until the marriage." She realized her mistake too late.

Thorpington brushed her words aside with an impatient gesture. "As for that, we shall see what marriage the future brings for Lady Isabella. I've a mind to wed that damsel myself."

Lady Almeria gasped. "*You* think to compete with *Dysart?*"

He smiled, self-satisfied. "I imagine my fortune will counteract his vaunted charm. Young ladies these days are far more practical than your romantic novels give them credit for."

"Go away," snapped Almeria, her own vaunted charm a casualty of her temper. "I wish to see no more of you."

He rose and bowed, but his smile remained. "As you will, cousin." He paused for a parting barb. "You might be interested to know that I expect soon to discover the whereabouts of the first earl's treasure."

This stopped her for a second, but she was made of sterner stuff. Her eyebrows raised only a trifle. "Indeed? May I ask how?"

He knew he had her. "Ah, that would be telling, would it not?"

"Rubbish," said Lady Almeria. "There is no treasure, or if there is, only the Old Gentleman would know where it lies."

"Exactly so." He bowed once more, and withdrew.

He was gone, but his essence yet polluted the bookroom. Almeria gave the portrait of her ancestor an apologetic look and smiled reassuringly. "No need to put yourself in a pucker, old Parsifal. That counter-coxcomb will never take over our home. If Eg and I have it in our power, Dysart will wed Isabella and all will come right. The gall of that clodpole, pretending to discern in your portrait a resemblance to himself! Imagine, Eustace as the seventh earl!"

The gigantic painting began to shudder, setting the objects on the mantelpiece to rattling against one another. It pulled away from the wall, hung ominously suspended for several long seconds, then pitched face forward onto the floor with a cataclysmic crash, sending china figurines and porcelain sheep ricocheting about the room like bird shot. The main workings of the French clock, which hadn't functioned for nearly a century, landed intact on one of the sofas.

Lady Almeria surveyed the debris with horrified dismay and reached for the bell-pull before she remembered that it, too, no longer worked.

The remains of the French clock musically struck thirteen and began to tick.

Was it, she wondered wildly, a good omen or an evil one?

# CHAPTER SIX

INCREDIBLY, THE PORTRAIT of the first Earl of Spadefield was undamaged. Thomas and Henry, Isabella's two footmen, directed by Creswell and aided by John Coachman, the stable-boy, and a man who had come to cart away the rubbish, managed to raise the immense painting. They hoisted it by means of creating pulleys with ropes run through the great hooks on the beam where the ceiling met the thick stone outer wall. The footmen each stood upon a ladder and succeeded at last, with no little difficulty, in reattaching the chains by which the heavy gilded frame was suspended above the chimneypiece.

The huge hooks, oddly enough, were unbent, and the chains untouched by the rust that should have accumulated in two centuries of contact with the ancient damp stone. There seemed no way the painting could have fallen, but by tacit agreement, no one speculated on the cause. Lady Almeria knew Parsifal would want his portrait replaced, so replace it they did. Once more the first earl aimed his supercilious gaze down at the occupants of the bookroom. As a last gesture, Almeria also replaced what was left of the French clock on the mantel. It was short one of the sheep, too shattered to mend, and also the heads of the shepherd and shepherdess. These she found under the furniture and set them on her desk to be glued back in place.

She then completed her note to dearest Maria Sefton and sent it by hand with Henry, the spriteliest of the footmen. Two of the new maids swept up the remaining debris which included the unfortunate porcelain sheep and the four china figurines which were no loss, being mere garish chimney ornaments from the factory in Stoke-on-Trent, Staffordshire. Spadefield House returned to normal. Or as normal as was possible.

Needless to say, the garrulous Mattie Ludd recounted the tale to Isabella with many embellishments that evening, arousing that lady's determination to meet in person with the spectre, but to Bella's disappointment, nothing untoward disturbed her night. In the morning, on her way to breakfast, she went first to the bookroom. The painted figure evinced no sign of sentience, the eyes staring blankly across at one of the shelves lined with volumes as though nothing had upset him. She entered the breakfast-room, bubbling over with questions.

Neither Lady Almeria nor Lady Eglantine seemed to feel that anything unusual had occurred, and they carefully steered the conversation away from the past evening's events. If they feared their ghost would frighten Bella into leaving, they were vastly mistaken!

"Let us drop the subject," Almeria said firmly when Bella demanded to be told the whole tale. "No harm done. Only a few paltry figurines, and in their place, we now have a clock that tells us the hour. It only wants a bit of glueing to be almost as good as new. Creswell will take care of it."

"But—" Bella began.

Lady Eg interrupted her. "Almeria, while we were in the Park yesterday, I discovered the perfect sire for Melisande's pups. Just the dog I have been searching for."

Bella still wanted to discuss searching for Parsifal's hoard. "But—" she began again.

Lady Almeria laid down her fork. "We prefer to ignore the Old Gentleman's peccadillos. It does not pay to stir him up."

Bella subsided, frustrated, and listened with half an ear to Lady Eg's version of the encounter in the Park.

"But I did not speak to her," Eg finished, buttering a muffin as though plastering a crack in its walls. "Is an opera dancer so very bad?"

Lady Almeria frowned. "One does not recognize the existence of females of that class."

"But we go to operas," Eg grumbled.

"One also goes to see the wild animals at the Exchange. However, one does not bring a beast into one's home."

"How am I to arrange for her dog to—"

"Good God, Eg! You cannot want a dog from that class."

Lady Eg swallowed a mouthful of her muffin. "There is no class where dogs are concerned. That is, breed and confirmation, of course, but their owners do not signify. Almeria, I have never seen such a dog..."

Or such an owner, Bella thought, remembering the redhead's confirmation. Really she could not wholly blame Chesney, but to drive the woman in the Park! She would not forgive Mr. Carlyle easily!

The ladies might not be willing to discuss Parsifal, but the sixth earl had no such compunctions. He wandered into the bookroom where the female members of the party forgathered after breakfast, as usual. He was full of his own theory, which also included Eustace Thorpington.

"A slap at the presumption of the man!" he exclaimed. "Only let me tell you of his doings the other night." He proceeded to regale them with the story of Mrs. Montfort's seance and Thorpington's part in it.

Bella's ears pricked up at the mention of Mr. Chesney Carlyle. How came he to be one of such a party? She knew a cold premonition. "This Mrs. Montfort, is she a, ah, that is, has she very red hair?"

Dysart looked at her, a strange reticence in his eyes. "As a matter of fact, she has."

Before Bella could speak again, Lady Eg broke in. "Dysart! Does this woman have a dog? A pug?"

"Why, yes. Attila. How did you know?"

Eg glanced quickly at her sister who was gathering herself for repressive speech. "No, no. I have not her acquaintance. It is only that I have seen her in the Park."

In Chesney's phaeton, Bella thought. How could she face Ches again without betraying her knowledge?

Dysart had returned to the topic of the seance and Thorpington's deceitful action.

"He was after Parsifal's treasure, mark my words. The fool thinks it is still here and that is why he's so anxious to get his grasping hands on Spadefield House. He no doubt plans to pull it down brick by brick and stone by stone. No wonder the Old Gentleman got so on his high ropes that he fell from his perch."

"Thorpington would be doomed to disappointment," said Lady Almeria. "There is no treasure."

Bella, alive with interest upon hearing that someone besides herself believed in the hidden hoard, tried to catch the portrait's painted eyes and could have sworn they twinkled as though the first earl were about to smile. When Dysart left the room, she made a casual excuse to run up to her chamber and instead cornered the sixth earl in the hall.

"Where does Parsifal go when he walks the halls?" she demanded. "I am sure if we but follow his path he would lead us to his hiding-place."

Dysart grinned, suddenly bearing an eerie resemblance to the portrait of his ancestor. "Do you plan a search, then? I wish you the best of luck. I have followed the sound of those ghostly footfalls and eerie clanks for years. Believe me, they lead one nowhere."

Bella was not to be put off. "Where is this nowhere?"

"Those who claim to have seen him say he takes the same route, along the third-floor corridor past the family bedrooms, down the great stairs to the kitchen premises, then up to the first storey where he crosses the ballroom to the point where the wall joins the West Tower. All sounds of footfalls and clanks then cease."

"The West Tower!" Bella bounced on her toes, clapping her hands. "That is where we must look!"

Dysart shook his head. "He couldn't have got inside there to hide anything. Those towers are part of the original structure and they were sealed up by Parsifal's great-grandfather when peace was declared between England and Scotland in 1491. The parsimonious old boy decided the elite corps of archers he kept to man the slit windows ate far more than the cost of their arrows and were no longer worth their keep. He bricked up the entrances to keep out thieves."

Bella was unwilling to give up this promising location and far from ready to drop the delightful subject of the spectre of Spadefield House, but at that moment a messenger came to the door and her quiet life changed.

The missive he brought contained the promise of the all-important voucher for Almack's, to be presented to Lady Isabella Greenlea after her Court Presentation.

"Dearest Maria!" Lady Almeria exclaimed. "She must have dispatched this directly upon receiving my note. Such gracious condescension! I must write her at once, and then we must see to Isabella's wardrobe for the coming balls and—Eg, we have not yet scheduled our own events! Quickly, find paper and quill—"

"Good Lord," said Dysart. "I'm off."

Bella giggled as he pretended to flee in terror, then had a presentiment she would soon wish to have done the same.

Almeria's note of thanks was sent post-haste and then, free of Dysart's masculine presence, the aunts plunged into an orgy of planning.

"The Court Presentation first and the come-out ball, then immediately after—start writing, Eg, do not be so slow—ridottos, drums and routs to meet the parents of all the young people."

"We must have a Venetian breakfast," put in Lady Eg, nibbling the feather end on her quill. "Alfresco parties."

"A musical soirée..."

Here Isabella felt obliged to put in a *non-placet*. "No, please. I neither play, nor sing to advantage."

"I'll cross that off then," agreed Eg. "But we must have an exploring picnic, Hampton Court?"

Lady Almeria gave such a sudden exclamation of horror that quill and paper flew from her sister's grasp and Melisande began to bark.

"*How* could we have been so remiss? We have not looked through your wardrobe, Isabella. We must do so at once to determine what must be procured."

"Indeed, I believe I have quite a number of gowns already. I brought three trunks, you know."

Almeria was hurrying up the stairs, talking as she went and trying not to trip over the excited pugs.

"Have your abigail lay out all for our inspection. Have you a bonnet for every gown? A cap or gauze head? You must not appear in public two days in a row in the same bonnet."

The profusion of garments spread out by Mattie Ludd were declared sadly lacking. Lady Almeria's eyes gleamed. "You will need a great deal more. Eg, we must purchase a copy of this year's *La Belle Assemblée*. I cannot imagine why we have not done so before."

Bella's head soon felt dizzy as the ladies rattled off the variety of gowns and wraps she would need: morning gowns, gowns for the opera, for promenading, the theatre, driving, riding, for dining, soirées, balls and the most extravagant of all, the Court

Presentation gown. For wraps she must have a Zephyr cloak, one of lace, Kashmir shawls, and mantles trimmed with fur, swansdown and marabou, all with gloves, slippers, half boots, muffs, reticules, fans and bonnet after bonnet to match.

Lady Almeria produced her last year's copy of *La Belle Assemblée or Lady's Fashionable Companion* and Isabella was temporarily distracted from Parsifal's treasure—as well as from Chesney and his flashy widow—at the sight of this fascinating volume. Eagerly, she unfastened the catch of the leather-bound pocketbook. Not French, as she had once believed, though still it relayed the latest news from the Continent. She had been disappointed to discover it was printed annually in London for the very British firm of Peacocks and Brompton, of Salisbury Square.

She began immediately to fold out and study the three-part pages of engravings depicting the latest styles. The pictured ladies, seated in theatrical settings or promenading in classical gardens, wore gowns much like those she had brought with her.

"*Passé,*" said Lady Almeria. "We must purchase the book for this year—or it will be far the best to go this very day to make the rounds of the most fashionable modistes in Town, for your father would wish you to be turned out in the first style of elegance."

She waved away Isabella's wardrobe with a dismissive gesture. "These will do well for morning wear or quiet dinners at home, but you will soon see there are significant changes in dress this year. Waists are even higher, skirts flare wider and all hems are decorated with flounces, garlands of flowers and knots of ribbon. Come, put on your pelisse and bonnet. We must go at once."

Since Viscount Robisham was franking all expenses, Lady Almeria recognized no limit to her purchases, and for the next few days poor Isabella's life became a mad round of milliners, mantua makers, caper merchants, and *coiffeurs*.

INTO THIS MAELSTROM, all unsuspecting, came Mr. Chesney Carlyle, bringing the Duke of Devron for a formal morning call. They were ushered ceremoniously into the bookroom where Lady Eglantine and Isabella were debating the merits of a Coburg bonnet or a Cossack hat to complement a warmly lined *douillette à la Russe* for driving out in colder weather. Devron was welcomed with all consideration due his rank, but Chesney found himself greeted with unexpected coldness by Bella, He puzzled over this while Lady Eglantine chattered to the duke.

"You find us two ladies quite alone. My sister is gone out and even Spadefield is from home, a most unusual circumstance these days while we harbour so enchanting a houseguest."

The duke bowed acknowledgement in Bella's direction. "Enchanting indeed!"

Ches knew he should be pleased to see Devron's pop-eyed gaze fixed on his young friend in blatant admiration. Why was he not? Of a certainty, this was what he had wished. And Bella, who seemed quite out of charity with himself, was putting forward her most charming manner towards the already infatuated duke. The chit was developing into a flirt! He should never have urged her to come to Town for the Season, not that his words ever had any influence on the actions of the wilful Isabella.

But to encourage such a court-card! For a moment, he had quite forgotten that Devron was here at his instigation. He recalled that fact, and began to doubt his reasoning. Seen in the daylight, and next to Bella's dewy freshness, the duke appeared older than he'd thought. "Appropriate age" should have been early among the qualifications on his list, although surely it was included under the ninth item, "Presentable." He admitted, with a tinge of annoyance, that he'd made an error.

He awoke from his musings to discover Lady Eglantine had turned the conversation to Bella's come-out ball and was assuring both they would soon receive their cards of invitation. A number of parties were being scheduled, and "Lady Isabella will be escorted by Spadefield, of course."

Were they being warned away? Ches wondered suddenly if only Dysart's aunts were in the scheme to acquire her fortune or if Viscount Robisham also had a marriage between his daughter and the dissolute earl in mind when he devised his plan of sending her to Spadefield House. He'd best have a serious talk with young Bella and while he was about it, drop a hint regarding her coquetry towards Devron.

The duke, who displayed a genuine fondness for pugs, admired Melisande and Terpsichore. Lady Eglantine, delighted, mounted her hobby-horse and commanded his complete attention, and Ches was enabled to speak with near privacy to Bella.

"My dear girl," he whispered, "from your behaviour, one would think you to be setting your cap at the duke."

A vivid flush rose on Bella's cheeks. "What can you mean? I am merely being polite to the gentleman."

"If that isn't just like you, Izzy. You've no more sense of propriety than the veriest schoolroom miss."

*Fighting words.* Ice formed on her next utterance. "Since when were you appointed arbiter of social deportment?"

He'd definitely chosen the wrong tack. Striving to reinstate friendly relations, Ches chose another topic, one sure to distract her. "Be that as it may. Tell me, have you as yet encountered the spectre?"

With the first sign of warmth she'd yet shown, Bella proceeded to tell him of the portrait of the first earl and its dramatic fall from the wall. "Because of Eustace Thorpington," she explained. "He had come to propose his purchase of Spadefield House, and naturally Parsifal felt the need to protest."

"Bosh," said Chesney.

"Bosh!" Bella exclaimed, indignant. "How else could it be?"

Ches smiled patiently as if she were a backward child. "My dear Izzy, this is an ancient house. No doubt the hooks that suspended it from the stone wall were weakened by rust from the dampness."

"They were clean! Strong as new, as were the chains that attached the heavy frame! I saw them myself."

Her eyes sparked in an uncomfortable manner, and Ches veered from the second unfortunate subject. "The weather is unusually clement, Bella. I wonder if you might give me the honour of driving you in Hyde Park this afternoon?"

For some odd reason, this simple request brought on a deluge of sleet to frost his notion of clement weather. The social rounds were about to start, she informed him. She was beset by mantua makers—she had no time for drives in the Park—and would not go if she had.

Ches shivered under the freezing onslaught. Plainly there was no pleasing the perverse chit today. He caught the eye of the duke, who by now must have learned a great deal more than he ever wished to know about the care of pugs in sickness and in health.

"I see we have come at a bad time," he informed Bella. "Pray excuse us. We shall take our leave at once."

"Do," said Bella, as chilly as from a dose of her own sleet.

Chesney parted from Devron at the door to Spadefield House, each heading towards more agreeable surroundings. Ches's temper was considerably bent. He refused to admit that his feelings were injured by Bella's coldness. *Just like all females,* he reasoned. Her only interests were in the style of her gowns and the figure she'd cut in the eyes of the haut ton. No time for old friends now. She was established in London... and in the society of persons of her own rank. In this mode, he soon worked himself into a state of righteous indignation.

Restless and at a loss for some activity to occupy his time until dinner, he remembered his intention to drive in the Park that afternoon. Mrs. Montfort had evinced great pleasure when he had driven her there a few days ago. Perhaps she would care to accompany him in his phaeton again. He determined to call on her later and extend the invitation.

Meanwhile, he headed towards the Daffy Club to blow a cloud and repair his damaged pride by downing a measure of Blue Ruin.

LADY ISABELLA WOULD HAVE had no taste for Blue Ruin, had she even known of it, and therefore had no way of appeasing her wrath. She was unable to rid her thoughts of Chesney's perfidy. First he drives his paramour in Hyde Park and then invites *her* to partake of the same occupation! And crowning all, to present to her the Duke of Devron, obviously in the guise of a candidate for her hand. Whatever was he about? Did he think to palm her off on that hoary old coxcomb—that...that pop-eyed, pear-shaped caricature of Prinny? Her lips tightened and a dangerous light gleamed in her eyes. She resolved to smile her brightest on the Earl of Spadefield, of whom Chesney did *not* approve.

# CHAPTER SEVEN

BELLA HAD NO TIME to further her plan of assault on Mr. Carlyle's bachelorhood, for at breakfast the next morning, Lady Almeria announced the imminent arrival of Madame Fleur d'Oreille d'Ours.

The name sounded highly improbable. "Who?" Isabella asked.

And "Who?" Lady Eg echoed.

Lady Almeria frowned at her sister. "You must recall, Eglantine. The modiste who designed the Court dress last year for Lady Bascombe's niece."

Eg was not a slowtop. "Ah," she said. "Two hundred pounds."

"Two hundred!" Bella exclaimed. "Surely ten times that amount! Of a certainty, my father would wish me to have an excessively elaborate gown for so important an occasion."

"And so you shall, my love." Almeria unfortunately sat too far from Eglantine to deliver her the sharp kick to the shin which she deserved. "I have not the slightest idea to what my sister refers. Your gown shall be the most elegant creation Madame can contrive."

The conversation went no further, for Creswell appeared at the door. "Madame d'Ours," he intoned. "I have placed her in the bookroom, my ladies." His expression indicated that in his judgement, modistes did not rate disturbing the pristine orderliness of the front drawing-room. The ladies, however, hastily dropped their forks and hurried into Madame's presence as though greeting royalty.

Even Bella was secretly impressed, her lips forming an awestruck *O*. Surely a modiste so elegant and so extravagantly French must be of the highest order. The madame's toilette, from bonnet to pointed toes, fairly shrieked *dans la haute société*, and when she spoke, her grammar and accent were indescribable.

Bella was led forward and presented with all the panoply of the prize heifer exhibited at a country fair, to which she had once likened her London debut.

"A complete new wardrobe," said Lady Almeria. "We place her entirely in your hands."

This, Bella soon discovered, was a patent falsehood. Lady Almeria remained determinedly in total charge. The bookroom became a theatre of spirited skirmishes, the air filled with a positive miasma of anglicized French.

Bella learned that Lady Almeria's favourite amaranthus was sadly out of fashion, as were the pomona and willow greens of the previous year. The coming colours were pistache, poussière, and even capucine.

"Coquelicot," pronounced Madame, "is of the fashionable still, but *not* for mademoiselle. For her the most delicate blush only, and *not* jonquil." She plucked at Bella's yellow flowered morning gown and shuddered, not unlike a jonquille in a stiff breeze. "Mademoiselle is of a fairness the most delightful. For her, we choose the blues: clarence, bishop's, or cerulean." She paused, a finger to her chin. "But not for the velvet pelisse, for that *poussière de Paris*."

The mention of velvet brought on a discussion of fabrics for Lady Isabella's ball gowns: *crêpe lisse, soie de Londres*, and spangled gauze to be edged with silver foil. They were off at once on trims: *torsades, rouleaux* of satin or gauze *bouillonnée*, with coquings or rosebuds and *noeuds* of nakara ribbon, *en carreaux, en serpent* or *en treilles*.

Lady Eg, not as fascinated by fashion's foibles as her sister, wisely refrained from taking part. She sat with her back turned, scrubbing Terpsichore's stomach. In near desperation, Bella sank onto an ottoman beside her.

"Why could we not employ an English modiste?" she whispered, under cover of a violent discussion that seemed to be about sleeves *en bouffes* or *bretelles*.

"Oh," said Lady Eg. "She *is* English."

"What!"

Eg cast a quick glance back as though to be sure she was unheard. "*Née* Mary Clarke," she said, sotto voce.

"Then why cannot she speak in plain English?" demanded Bella, indignant.

"Impossible," Eg explained. "The best modistes always speak of fabrics and colours in French. Otherwise, we would know what she was talking about and would not be willing to pay such outrageous prices for common pink or white silk."

Lady Almeria called the meeting sharply to order. All this discussion of detail could wait until the morrow.

"Of first importance," she declared, "is the Court dress for Isabella's Presentation."

This brought on another flood of French, from which Madame emerged victorious. Isabella must be garbed in bride-colours of pale blue, silver and white. "She will bloom as a luminous orchid among the bed of garden lilies. Now to work! To work!"

The project went into production at once, and to her dismay, Bella learned that the huge hoop skirt was still *de rigueur* for this premier event, even in this year of 1815.

"I'll look a perfect quiz!" she exclaimed.

Lady Almeria was firm. "So will all the others, so let us have no nonsense."

For the next few days, Bella was overwhelmed by the arguments and discussions over the design of her gown and the accompanying furbelows, the necessary number of plumes for her headdress, the width of the paniers and by the ells of satin, lace and gauzy tulle draped over her wilting figure through the interminable fittings.

Spadefield House resembled a florist's shop—or possibly a funeral parlour—as flowers arrived daily from the Duke of Devron, and from Eustace Thorpington, who had got wind of the duke's interest and had no intention of being cut from the running before he made the lady's acquaintance. This would have to be later, for Creswell had taken pleasure in informing him that Lady Almeria had given instructions that no callers were to be admitted to Spadefield House. The ladies were not at home until after Lady Isabella's Presentation.

Several times Mr. Chesney Carlyle was announced and hastily turned away with apologies by Lady Almeria. This was no time for visits with old friends from home. Dysart, who knew better, played least in sight, and eventually Chesney formed a tentative alliance with him. Somehow both gentlemen spent a great deal of their time with Mrs. Fanchette Montfort. That wise lady held herself always available.

As the great day neared, the tumult and tension in Spadefield House grew apace. Lady Eg kept out of the way, holing out in the bookroom like a wary hedgehog and snoring rhythmically in her padded chair before the fire. The whistling wheeze of grey-muzzled Terpsichore, asleep in her lap, accompanied her snorts in a musical descant.

Melisande, bored and feeling neglected, tired of sitting on the floor and watching them. She pattered up the stairs in search of livelier companionship. Drawn to the bedroom corridor by the sounds of commotion and voices from the chamber occupied by their guest, Melisande perked up. This new young lady knew exactly how to scratch behind her ears and was always ready to oblige. The door stood open and she peered round its bottom corner.

The prospects for ear scratching did not appear good. Lady Almeria was there, as well as the guest and her abigail, all three waving gowns and petticoats. Ordinarily, Melisande would have joined happily in what seemed to be a romp, but then she saw the feathers on the floor.

The fact that these feathers were partially wrapped in silver paper bearing the imprint of Mr. Carberry, London's foremost plumier, in no way concerned Melisande. Feathers were feathers, and with no bonnet attached, feathers meant a bird. She knew better than to attack feathers on bonnets. Three disastrous attempts to slay such during her puppy years had made this difference quite clear. But these feathers, as she had noted, had no bonnet. At long last, after nearly giving up all hope, she was about to catch a bird. Her tongue lolled and she drooled.

Latent jungle instincts pulsed through her veins. The occupants of the room had not seen the bird. It sat quietly, waiting. Melisande pulled in her tongue lest she should accidentally bite it, and crept through the door. Grovelling on her tummy, her legs spread out flat, she crawled with swimming motions across the carpet and behind a chair. The bird didn't move; it hadn't seen her. Gathering herself together for one triumphant leap, she let out a coloratura war cry and pounced.

She seized the pile of feathers by what she hoped was the neck and proceeded to shake the life from it. She almost succeeded before pandemonium struck.

Directly below, Terpsichore was dumped onto the floor as a series of furious shrieks penetrated the bookroom. Lady Eg flew into the hall, to be greeted by the sight of a wild-eyed Melisande bounding down the stairs, trailing a pale blue ostrich plume from her teeth. Behind the pug came Mattie Ludd, armed with the hearth broom, then Almeria, closely followed by Isabella. The parade, with the exception of Bella, who collapsed on the stairs doubled up with laughter, rounded the landing and headed on down. Eg took in the situation at a glance. Catching up her skirts, she galloped after Melisande, going to the rescue of her beloved pug.

Already at the foot of the stairs, she was front runner and reached Melisande first, scooping the excited dog into her protective arms. She extracted what was left of the plume and handed it to her sputtering sister. Then, cowardly, she fled.

A short time later, a startled Creswell, retiring to his still-room for a soothing glass of port before the preparation for tea, found the refugees in hiding. Lady Eg set down her liberal sampling of his best vintage.

"Hoy, Creswell," she whispered. "Any sign of my sister without?"

Ever the perfect butler, he regained his composure. "No, my lady. I believe her to be in Lady Isabella's chambers."

"Good." Eg kept her voice cautiously lowered. Almeria's ears were sharp. It seemed best to remove both Melisande and herself, and it was, after all, the hour for a fashionable drive in Hyde Park. "Send word to John Coachman to bring the barouche to the kitchen door."

Creswell maintained his wooden countenance. "Yes, my lady."

Eg fixed him with a steady stare. "I feel the need of a drive in the Park." She tossed off her port with debonair grace. "Fresh air," she explained.

"Yes, my lady."

"And you might ask Mrs. Creswell to pop up to my room and bring down my lavender pelisse and the matching Coburg."

"Yes, my lady."

"And do stop saying 'Yes, my lady' in that infernally insufferable manner. Hop it, Creswell."

Half an hour later, seated in the open barouche, Lady Eglantine and Melisande were driven through the gates of Hyde Park. They were somewhat late. Several other carriages were already on the way out; one of them she recognized as Mr. Chesney Carlyle's phaeton. Beside him sat the female with the flaming red hair, and on her lap she held the "Magnificent Dog."

They were leaving the Park and no doubt on their way to that woman's home. Eg gripped her parasol, her knuckles white. She could discover where to find that pug!

Scrambling up onto the forward seat, she leaned as far as she could and poked John Coachman in the back with the ferrule of the parasol.

"Follow that phaeton!" she commanded.

THE GRAND Court Presentation was arranged for a Thursday, and the date and Bella's gown arrived so nearly together that Lady Almeria came close to apoplexy. Only the sight of the carriage pulling up, piled high with huge boxes from Madame, saved her from succumbing to a near-fatal fit of the vapours.

Bella had seen the basic parts of her ensemble during the many fittings, but now she was to see it complete with every final embellishment in place. She stared, open-mouthed but speechless, as Lady Almeria and Mattie Ludd opened the boxes one by one and lifted a faery-like concoction from the mounds of silver paper. First a cloud of ostrich feather plume, then the pearl-covered bodice and the skirts—layers of silken satin, silver-shot lace and spangled gauzy tulle.

There was barely time for Bella to don the entire regalia. It would take hours. Lady Almeria stood her upon a low stool so her dressers could circle round her. The hoop skirt, of waxed calico stiffened with whalebone, was tied about her waist. It swayed dangerously when she attempted to look down at her feet.

"I shall never be able to manage this!" Bella complained.

"You shall," said Lady Almeria. "You must. Here, step down and take a few minutes to walk about the room. No, no, do not pace so. Tiny steps. You must set up a rhythm swinging the hoop paniers ever—no! Try again."

Bella tried, and after a few minutes Almeria decided she had mastered the knack and returned her to the stool.

An interruption occurred. The coiffeur had arrived to fashion her hair. He was very nearly as French as Madame and, Bella suspected, also from Liverpool or Smithfield or the Metropolis. The magnificent plumed headdress designed by Madame had to be displayed for his inspection. Mr. Carberry had delivered a new supply of feathers in multiple shades of blue, sending the hairdresser into raptures.

He dressed Bella's hair in the latest French style, a profusion of curls coaxed down about her cheeks, the hindermost hair piled high to be partly concealed by the headdress. At the front the tresses were divided in the centre to bare her forehead in order to display a diamond-and-pearl bandeau set very low above her eyebrows.

Seeing the feathers reminded Bella of Melisande, currently locked in Creswell's pantry for safety. She tried to catch Lady Eg's eye. That lady had been very silent so far and Bella, looking at her sharply to see why she took no part, was surprised by the oddity of her expression. Lady Eg seemed miles away, and she smiled in a most peculiar fashion.

"Why is she looking so... so smug?" Bella asked aloud.

Lady Almeria had no time for the vagaries of her eccentric sister. The coiffeur was dismissed until he was needed to add the headdress. "Now for the gown," she told Bella. "Back to the stool. Hand me the petticoat, Ludd."

This first layer was of celestial blue satin, matching the bodice, finished at the hem with silver vandyke trim below a garlanded wreath of *gofre crape* roses in blues and white against a wide band of silver lamé.

A second skirt followed, shorter than the petticoat, of silver-shot white lace caught up in flounces headed by *rouleaux* of pale blue zephyrine twisted with a rope of pearls.

With the aid of Mattie Ludd, Lady Almeria eased the bodice over Bella's head. It was of pale blue satin, stitched with pearls *en treillis* and edged with a wreath of silver net lozenges, each formed by a circle of pearls, above silver vandyke trim. The sleeves, barely touching her shoulders, were *en bouffes*, very short puffs of the blue satin overlaid with lace interspersed with pearls laid on in waves. From the tips of her shoulders a full Elizabeth ruff of silver tissue dotted with more pearls stood up high around the back of her neck. The corsage was so tiny that Bella eyed it anxiously and tried to pull it up a trifle, but Lady Almeria slapped at her hand.

"Do not touch *anything!*" she ordered.

"But I shall surely come out if I but turn only slightly!"

"You will have no call to turn. You will walk in straight forward, make your curtsies and then back away."

The final skirt, the *pièce de résistance* was of spangled blue tulle. The shortest of all, it was tucked up in great scallops festooned with silver ribbon and each tuck held in place with a nosegay of blue roses, pink rosebuds, and delicate palmated green leaves set in a silver lace ruffle.

The coiffeur stepped forward once more, and handling it as though it were a royal crown, he placed the headdress on Bella's curls. The profusion of blue feathers rose from a mass of diaphanous white gauze gleaming with diamond buckles and held in place with diamond combs. A flock of *ailes de papillon*, silver foil butterflies, were made to hover about her head.

Bella stared into her mirror. "Good heavens," she murmured. "Must I wear so many feathers?"

"There are barely a dozen. You shall see many like this on other ladies; some may have at least two dozen."

"Why? Sheer ostentation?"

"No, no. Merely to take the eye from an unfortunate cast of features. You have no need for such subterfuge and will do very well with less."

"So I should hope! I shall have the headache as it is."

The final accoutrements were now added: white satin slippers with rosettes of pearls and diamond buckles, long white kid gloves embroidered in silver thread and a silver-and-white chicken-skin fan, each blade tipped in marabou and blue ostrich feathers. A place was found on her person for every jewel she possessed.

Bella stood back and gazed at herself in the mirror once more.

"I must appear a raree from a side-show!" she exclaimed.

Lady Eg had awakened from her trance. "Of course you do," she said. "Whatever made you think you were attending anything but?"

Her sister frowned. "Really, Eg! This is a once-in-a-lifetime event and must be given every mark of distinction. You would not wish our Isabella to appear a dowd."

"A dowd!" Bella tried to shake her head but found it too top-heavy to risk the movement. "A dowd, indeed. In masquerade, perhaps. May I not wear a loo-mask? I vow, if I meet an acquaintance, I shall not know which way to look."

"You look exquisite, my love. Certain to cast all others in the shade. No one will have a toilette such as yours."

"Indeed, I should hope not."

"You'll see when you arrive." Lady Eg patted her arm, reassuring her. "You'll not be in the least out of place."

"Good God!" Lady Almeria cried suddenly. "Look at the hour! We have as yet to dress ourselves."

Adjuring Mattie Ludd to see that her mistress neither sat nor leaned against something but stood perfectly still until the carriage came, the ladies rushed off to make their own hasty toilettes.

Bella turned carefully back to her mirror. She had to admit the effect, though bizarre, was vastly becoming. The silken blue satin of the corsage, threaded with softly gleaming pearls, brought out the delicate cream and peach of her complexion. The repeated blues of the soft ostrich feathers curling about her head turned her hair to burnished gold. If only Ches could see her in this fantasy regalia. He'd soon realize she was no longer the little country miss he thought her. But there was no chance of that. Mr. Chesney Carlyle would not be called upon to attend a Queen's Drawing-room. And if he should be, he would not go, saying there was some mistake for he had not sufficient *rank*. Oh, d-drat Ches and his idiotic pride!

IN DEFERENCE to her wide hoop and elaborate gown, Isabella rode to Court in a closed carriage rented for the occasion. She travelled alone but for Mattie Ludd, who sat on the edge of the forward seat, hovering like a fussy sparrow with her first nestling. Bella's two footmen, Thomas and Henry, perched outside on the bench behind, resplendent in the lavish Robisham livery, with monstrous bouquets in their lapels. Following in the barouche, their only carriage, were Lady Almeria and Lady Eglantine, dressed to the nines.

The general hysteria of nerves had communicated to Bella. She sat dry-mouthed, clutching her silver-embroidered fan so tightly that one of the ivory vanes cracked with an audible snap. She leapt as though stung, striking her towering plumage on the roof of the carriage.

Mattie Ludd squeaked in horror. "My lady! You've never ruined it?"

Bella felt the base of her headdress, her hands shaking. All seemed securely anchored. "It depends," she said. "Do you mean my feathers or my fan?"

Mattie inspected both. The ostrich feathers, fortunately, were fresh and springy. The fan was another matter.

"You'll have to leave it shut, my lady, for it now sags in the middle."

A nervous giggle escaped from Bella. "I'm sure I'll find no reason to flirt with it at this affair."

Mattie frowned. "Indeed not, my lady. And it's no place for kicking up one of your larks," she added severely.

Bella giggled again, this time oddly relieved by Mattie's manner returning her to the schoolroom. With the aunts both in a dither, she had been feeling rather lost and welcomed a figure of authority. Now she would survive if only nothing else went wrong.

For some little time, nothing did. The parade of carriages inched its way along Piccadilly towards St. James's Palace. Finally, after seeming hours, it was Bella's turn to alight at the entrance. Thomas and Henry jumped down, one to open the carriage door, the other to let down the steps.

Bella took a deep breath and rose, crouching to protect her plumes as she ducked under the low roof. She extended one foot towards the top step and attempted to descend gracefully. Then, in spite of all the careful instruction by Lady Almeria in the management of the awkward contrivance, she jammed her hoop in the door of the carriage.

She could neither move forward nor backward. A slight struggle brought only the tiny sound of tearing fabric, and she froze. Thomas and Henry gaped up at her.

"Good heavens," she whispered. "I do believe I am stuck."

She was. Both footmen leapt to her aid but, terrified of hearing more rents, she pushed them away. Behind her, Mattie caught at her waist and tried to pull. The long parade of arrivals drew to a halt far back up the road and irate coachmen could be heard shouting. The Ladies Almeria and Eglantine tumbled from the barouche, rushing to see what had happened. Isabella could hear, echoing in her mind, Chesney's exasperated voice. *"Izzy, if this is not just like you. You have no more decorum than a schoolroom miss!"*

"I *knew* I'd make a mull of it," she wailed as the aunts came up. "I dare not move for fear I'll ruin my gown!"

"Stand perfectly still," Almeria ordered, taking charge at once. "You, Ludd, back there, see if you can bend the skirt in—gently—that's right. Now, Bella, while I push in this side and Eg the other— bend the back in more, Ludd—there, now, you are free."

Bella stood on the cobbles at last, the footmen climbed back up to their bench and the carriage moved on to a chorus of vulgar shouts from the coachmen behind. Her hoop was bent and her plumes knocked sadly askew, giving her a rather demented appearance. "Am I ruined?" Bella, cast into the greatest affliction, blinked back tears. "I have finished us all!"

"No, no." Lady Almeria pushed her to one side to allow the next carriage to disgorge its satin-and-jewelled passengers. "We'll have you to rights in a moment." She began adjusting the headdress while Lady Eg and Mattie straightened the bent hoop as well as they could.

"Oh, dear, what will Her Majesty think of me?" Bella mourned."

She need not have worried. No one girl would ever be remembered in the crush that greeted her inside. They found the reception room in which she was to wait crowded with hoop-skirted young ladies, their mamas and attendants. Bella gazed at a veritable sea of undulating ostrich plumes and her stomach, already queasy, began to send clear signals of *mal de mer*.

Two full hours passed with Bella standing on aching feet, filled with longing thoughts of chairs and fresh air. Overcome by the heat, her tight stays and an excess of excitement, she feared she might swoon. She had no need. On the far side of the room, another overwrought young lady fainted for her. Immediately, the girl was imitated by others all around Bella. The sharp odours of vinaigrettes and sal volatile filled the close air, mingling with every imaginable fragrance of the perfumiers. Isabella had eaten no lunch—for which she would be eternally thankful—and managed to force down her nausea before she embarrassed herself and the aunts, and incidentally ruined a thousand pounds worth of billowing tulle and pearl-studded satin.

Her name was finally announced. Lady Almeria guided her towards the great double doors leading to the Queen's Drawing-room, Lady Eg preceding, clearing a way. Bella paused on the threshold. The long room swam in a hazy blur of faces lining a strip of carpet down which she had to walk.

She tried desperately to remember Lady Almeria's instructions. Curtsy at the door. Step through and curtsy again. Then down the endless gauntlet of haughty ladies and quizzing glassed gentlemen towards the pair of high gilded chairs on the raised dais at the far end of the room. Numb with fatigue and blind to all but the danger of tripping over her own feet and probably losing control of her bent hoops, she moved ahead.

Somehow she reached the dais and curtsied once more. Raising her eyes from the floor as she straightened carefully upright, she took her first look at royalty in the flesh.

The aging queen, short, fat, bewigged and bejewelled, was flanked by her eldest son, the once-charming Prince Florian of a decade before. Bella recognized him immediately from the unflattering political cartoons with which she was familiar, though his resemblance to Devron startled her. She was definitely not impressed by the corpulent, pop-eyed Prince Regent, who nodded to her with bored indifference while inhaling an enormous pinch of snuff. She made her final curtsy with surprising ease and backed away.

After all the fuss and bother and expense of the past few weeks, it was over within minutes!

And for *this* she had left Chesney Carlyle exposed to the wiles of that redheaded female... with who knew what fatal results.

# CHAPTER EIGHT

MR. CHESNEY CARLYLE, seated at breakfast in his lodgings off St. James's Street, was in a thoughtful mood. This past week, he had been repeatedly refused admittance to Spadefield House by Lady Almeria. Having no knowledge of the time-consuming and all-important business of preparing a young lady for her formal Presentation, he was at a loss to understand why he was considered an unwelcome guest. More and more, he became convinced that Viscount Robisham and the Westphale ladies were in league to wed Bella to Dysart. Such a marriage would never do! The sixth Earl of Spadefield fell far short in his list of requirements for a *parti* for Lady Isabella Greenlea.

Suddenly needing reassurance, he pulled the list from his pocket and smoothed its creases. He consulted it a trifle anxiously, seeing the earl earned two points at once for rank and undeniably excellent lineage. Of the next item on the list, honour, he remained doubtful. True, Dysart had expressed repugnance at the idea of marrying for a fortune, but he had shown signs of yielding to pressures from his aunts. Put him one down.

A man of fashion? Yes, but wealth drew a decided no. Even points there, cancelling each other. Consequence? An earl held a certain position as a Peer of the Realm, but surely Dysart's reputation countered that. Even again, but he was still one up owing to rank.

What else? Disposition. He had discovered the man to be the best of company for a night on the Town, ever amenable to suggestion and meeting adversity at the gaming table with unfailing good humour, but were these qualities to please a lady? Ches's innate sense of fair play made him hesitate before striking off this point. He had to admit that he'd surely seen the earl at his worst and found nothing about the man to cause disgust. Drinking to excess he did not consider a serious fault, he himself being sometimes guilty there. Reluctantly, he awarded a half point.

Only one and a half so far. But intelligence and presentability—now including proper age—gave Dysart two more. Three and a half. *Not enough.*

With a grim sense of satisfaction, Ches perceived it as his duty to scotch the plans of father and godmother at once. But how? Bella was by far too contrary to listen to any advice he might offer. That left Dysart. And the earl, he remembered, was enamoured of the Widow Montfort. There, then, was the crack into which to insert his wedge.

But much depended on the attitude of the lady herself. At the seance, he had detected a decided warmth in her manner towards the earl. *How* warm were her feelings was a thing he must ascertain at once. A glance at his clock on the mantel caused him to push away the remains of a plate of rare beef and gulp down the last of his ale. If he hurried, he could reach Clarges Street in proper time for a morning visit.

He had by now attended three of her card parties and driven her twice in the Park at the fashionable hour of five. Mrs. Fanny Montfort, he had found, was a needle-witted woman surviving by her canniness, and one who knew exactly how to entertain a gentleman. She should deal well with the rackety Earl of Spadefield. As Ches had always been in more than comfortable circumstances himself, Dysart's lack of ready blunt never crossed his mind. The earl's rank should please the widow. She would enjoy being a countess. On this comforting conclusion, he hailed a hackney and soon was deposited at the lady's doorstep.

The maid who served at the card parties recognized him and admitted him to the widow's presence at once. With a delighted cry, Mrs. Montfort fluttered to her feet from behind a writing desk scattered with letters, bills, quills, wafers and inkpots.

Involuntarily, Ches caught his breath at the picture she presented. Her glowing hair was brushed into a riot of burnished ringlets and her astonishing figure displayed to perfection in a soft cotton twill round gown, wood-block printed in a flattering olive-and-yellow flower pattern. A veritable model, he thought, bemused, for a Goddess of Plenty.

She greeted him effusively. "Mr. Carlyle! Well come indeed, luv. You rescue me from a most dreary morning!"

Taken aback, Ches hesitated, "luv" not being the form of address he expected. But perhaps, owing to the widow's open nature and vast acquaintance, it was not a term meant seriously. He had sometimes noticed a subtle want of delicacy in her manner. Making a graceful bow over the fingertips she offered, he omitted to kiss them though she managed to seize his hand and press it. Extricating himself, he gestured towards the untidy writing desk.

"I hope I do not interrupt an important task."

"No, no. It is a pleasure to be interrupted. Such a worrisome business, totting up one's debts and coping with creditors."

She now caught both his hands and pulled him over to a sofa. "Come, let us be comfortable. I do not stand upon ceremony, such good friends as we are."

She seated herself beside him and began to talk at once, while he perched uneasily on the edge of the cushions. It was enough to cast one into high fidgets to sit so close to her, alone in the privacy of her parlour.

"Cheer me up, do," she begged. "Settling up with one's creditors is such a plaguey nuisance. I vow, if things do not change soon, I shall be in the devil of a hobble if not actually in dun territory."

Ches felt mildly surprised. Surely, he was surrounded by opulence: gleaming mahogany, velvet draperies and an excellent Axminster at his feet. She must have read his thoughts from the expression on his face, for she went on quickly.

"You must know, my husband left his estate in the most stupid way. I have only the merest widow's mite paid quarterly and must rely totally upon the earnings of this house which, I promise you, barely suffice. You can have no notion of the expense of running an establishment of this sort. Only see—" She bounced up and retrieved a handful of bills from the desk. Returning to her place on the sofa, rather closer to Ches than before, she began to count them off.

"This from Priddy's Foreign Warehouse and vaults, twelve dozen of Fine Hock at thirty shillings the dozen, twelve dozen of Claret, First Growth, at forty-two shillings a dozen and the same of Champagne at seventy. And for my suppers, salmon mayonnaise and green peas in the amount of eighty pounds! I would not have thought it possible for these charges to total so much, but then I daresay they are not correct. I am only a defenceless widow, alone and lonely, on whom everyone may impose."

Playing the helpless female with consummate skill, she tried to smile and dabbed at her eyes with a scrap of lace. "I beg of you, my dear sir, forget my fustian nonsense. I'll say no more on this head."

It was an awkward situation. Cudgelling his brain for something to say, Ches remembered his intention to drive her in the Park. It seemed highly inadequate as a palliative for such excessive woe, but to his amazement his suggestion met with instant success.

"Just the thing!" she exclaimed, radiant once more. "How I have been longing for such an excursion to clear my poor head."

On this happier note, Ches managed to take his leave, promising to return for her later that afternoon. Her tale of deprivation and loneliness had aroused his sympathy towards a gentle female in the toils of adversity. Quite overset, he left Clarges Street much exercised in his mind and having quite forgotten his purpose to sound out the widow regarding her feelings for the sixth earl.

Blinded by his innate sense of chivalry, he also failed to see the jaws of the trap that were closing about him.

BOTH LADY ALMERIA and Isabella kept to their rooms that morning, exhausted after Bella's Presentation. Lady Eg, quite as exercised in her mind as Chesney but for a very different reason, wandered from room to room, trailed by Melisande. She counted on her fingers. Melisande was coming increasingly closer to her "time" and as yet no contact had been made with that magnificent pug. Attila. The name suited so redoubtable a dog; she'd thought so at once when Dysart dropped the name of the pug in her presence, accidentally betraying his intimacy with the redheaded female.

And she knew where Attila resided. She hugged that knowledge to herself.

Left on her own, she had a sudden urge to go out in the carriage. To drive aimlessly about the streets of London—or so John Coachman must think—and perhaps, just perhaps, travel down Clarges Street. Creswell chose that moment to cross the hall and she sent him to summon the barouche.

All was yet quiet abovestairs. She hardly expected to see the others until a late nuncheon would be spread in the breakfast room, and Terpsichore snored peacefully in her basket. The way was clear. Eg scooped up Melisande and slipped out of the house.

After directing John Coachman round a number of seemingly random turns, she felt a tingling awareness along her spine as they reached Clarges Street. The barouche, the horses ambling along, proceeded slowly past a small square containing a little park fenced in ornamental iron. And in that park, a pug dog romped through the shrubbery chasing pigeons. Eg let out her breath in a long, satisfied sigh. Attila.

He was not alone. On one of the benches, a footman, his chin on his chest, slept the sleep of the unobserved domestic. The man snapped awake as the door to the house opposite was opened. Eg hunched down in her seat as they passed, for she recognized the man who strode down the steps. Eustace Thorpington. He walked off in the other direction and she settled back, her mind relieved of her two most pressing anxieties. She knew where to find that pug without his mistress's knowledge, and with that mistress occupying Thorpington's leisure hours, they need have no fear of his pursuing Dysart's Lady Isabella.

A daring scheme began to evolve in her devious mind, and she directed John Coachman to head for home. If the pug Attila was allowed to run in the little park mornings, and the footman took advantage of his dog-minding duty to nap, why, would it not be an easy matter to insert Melisande into that park on a vital day and let nature take its course?

SHORTLY AFTER Lady Eg's departure, Bella, with the resilience of youth, wandered down the grand staircase and into the bookroom. She gazed up at the first Earl of Spadefield whose painted eyes stared into space. The moon not being full, Parsifal remained secluded in whatever after-world he existed. He made Bella feel guilty.

"I do beg your pardon," she apologized aloud. "I have not intentionally ignored you this week, it is just that everything came to a halt over that silly Presentation."

Parsifal showed no response, and she meandered over to the writing desk where Lady Almeria kept invitations and the cards of visitors. It had been several days, she realized, since Chesney Carlyle had called. Not only Parsifal had been ignored. She remembered Lady Almeria had turned Ches away more than once during the frenetic gown fittings, and her stomach gave a sudden lurch. What must he have thought! Coldness clutched at her chest. She turned back to the portrait, needing to speak to someone—anyone.

"I may have lost him forever to that red-haired creature. What shall I do?" she begged the painted figure. "At your age, you must have had a deal of experience with this sort of thing."

She expected no answer but—she looked at the portrait closely. Surely, Parsifal's expression had changed!

His painted eyes had become fixed to something across the room. She followed the path which seemed to lead to a shelf of books—he had done that before—at one book in particular? The row held contemporary fiction, novels belonging to Lady Eg— and in the midst, a volume on architecture strangely out of place. She drew it out with a hand that had begun to tremble.

Curling up in Lady Eg's chair before the hearth, she opened the book and began to turn the pages. They flipped through her fingers, inexplicably stopping at an engraving of a spiral flight of steps. Could this be a sending? A message from the world beyond the grave? She glanced up at Parsifal. His spectral eyes seemed to look straight into hers and she was fleetingly aware of a distinct resemblance between the Old Gentleman and Dysart in one of his teasing moods. Dysart. Of course. She had already decided the sixth earl was the most important weapon of her arsenal in the battle for Ches's surrender. Parsifal must mean she should enlist Dysart's aid to awaken jealousy in Mr. Chesney Carlyle's elusive heart. And what better way to create intimacy with Dysart than to involve him in an all-about search for Parsifal's lost treasure?

She looked again at the picture of the spiral stairs and her pulse began to race. How else would one climb a round tower? The West Tower! She shivered with anticipation and raised her eyes to Parsifal.

"Thank you," she whispered, and could swear he winked. The flicker—if there really was one—occupied less than an instant and she couldn't be sure.

Four storeys of Spadefield House abutted the West Tower and she was uncertain which rooms to search, for the tower itself she estimated to be fifty or sixty feet in diameter. Perhaps the archers had slept in the attics and could have entered the top of the tower directly. She grinned up at Parsifal. Dysart would know.

The sixth earl had not yet left his chambers—which, incidentally, adjoined the inside wall of the tower. The master's suite—might not there be an entrance there? Meanwhile, until she could ask him in person, she began her own search on the ground floor.

She was kneeling, tapping the wainscotting in the front drawing-room and listening for a hollow sound, when Lady Almeria spoke behind her. "Are you emulating Eustace Thorpington, Isabella? I assure you, he has already tried that."

Bella sat back on her heels, unembarrassed. "There must be a secret passageway into the tower. I mean to discover it."

Lady Almeria smiled, shaking her head. "You might as well give up. Sounding the walls is a hopeless task in so ancient a building. They are of stone, you must know, six feet and more in thickness. There would be nothing in the tower. It has been sealed off for hundreds of years." She spread her hands. "The Old Gentleman could not have got in to hide his treasure. I fear I have come to agree with Dysart, for Parsifal was not known to be insane. Believe me, he absconded and took every dratted valuable in the place with him."

Bella let the matter drop. It was, after all, Dysart she wished to involve and she waited her chance.

Typical of London weather, it came on to a pouring rain that evening. Luckily, no engagement had been planned, the ladies fully expecting to be worn to flinders after the Presentation. In the bookroom, Lady Almeria sat nodding over Mrs. Radcliffe's latest novel. Terpsichore snored in her basket by the fire. Lady Eg cuddled Melisande in her lap, her eyes unfocussed, gazing into some wondrous dreamland while her lips moved as though she worked over some tremendous escapade in her mind.

Dysart joined them after dinner and paced restlessly beneath Parsifal's portrait, even he hesitating to venture forth into the storm.

Now. Bella rose from the hassock where she had been pretending to read a book, unaware she held it upside down. She set the novel down on the table and taking the architectural volume from its place on the shelf, she drew the sixth earl to the far end of the room.

"Dysart, I need your help. I am going to search for Parsifal's treasure."

He patted her on the head kindly. "Nay, child. A waste of time."

Child. Bella set her lips. Truly, he was as bad as Ches. "I have a feeling your fortune is still here, and Parsifal wants it found. Only look at this." She produced the book, opened to the picture of the spiral staircase, and told him how she came upon it.

He gave her an odd look. "Straight from the Old Gentleman himself, eh? Now why would he do that? Why you? Why not one of his descendants who've been searching for the past two hundred years?"

"Perhaps I am the first to really believe he still exists, the only one who believes in *him* and is not hunting his treasure for sheer greed."

Interest flared in Dysart's eyes. "Damme, you may be right. Lead on, my lady, and let us hope he does not consider me one of the greedy ones. What had you in mind, for I am sure I detect a scheme afoot?"

"First, tell me, is there such a flight of steps in Spadefield House? In the West Tower, perhaps? It is into that wall that your spectre is said to disappear."

"We must go to the muniment room," he said decisively. "It is in the East Tower, and that tower may be a replica of the other. We may find the original building plan there." Now it was he who hurried her out into the hall. "Wait here, I must get a key from Creswell." He returned within a few minutes with a large, rusty iron key and two lit candlesticks.

They made their way through a series of unused rooms, the ghostly shapes of furniture draped in holland covers looming out of the darkness like spirits rising up around them. Bella firmly suppressed an urge to cling to the earl's arm like a timid Bath miss.

At the other side of the house, Dysart stopped before a heavy oaken door. She held his lighted candle as well as her own while he struggled with the ancient lock.

"No one's been in the east wing since my father died." He told her. "My grandfather used this for his library, but it was too cold and damp for my governor. And it's too costly to keep so much of the house open. When my aunts came, we moved to the west side over the servants' quarters to save heat and candles."

He gave a great heave and the door creaked open. The room beyond exuded a musty odour like the opening of a tomb. Bella shivered as he took back his candle.

"No hearth in here—sorry. These towers were originally for defence and my ancient ancestors could see no reason to keep their archers warm and drowsy. They wanted them alert."

Bella shivered again. "I should think their fingers would be too frostbitten to draw their bows."

"Indeed. Just as well they were forced to seek warmer employment." He crossed the darkened room. Dust motes, stirred to action by the unaccustomed draft, sparkled in the wavering light of his candle. "Come on in, but take care, it is probably full of spiders." He grinned wickedly. "Best stay close beside me. More than spiders may haunt this tower."

Only too true! The flickering candles seemed to draw wraiths and spectres from shadows that filled the room, roiling like smoke on the edge of her vision, vanishing when she tried to look at them. Far more terrifying, small, dark shapes rustled and scurried for cover beyond the pools of light.

Bella lifted her chin. "I am not one afraid of spiders," she lied.

"Or ghosts? They say the Old Gentleman only walks at the full moon, but my grandfather claimed to have seen him once during a raging storm. Probably much like this one. And in this very room."

"I do not fear him, either, so you have no need to put your arm about me."

"You cannot fault me for trying." He removed the offending arm. "However, I fancy we should have brought Melisande for the rats."

Bella caught up her skirts nervously and stared about. Her candle passed over carved chests, a solid, cross-beamed trestle table, chairs so covered with dust that she could not divine the colours or patterns of the tapestry seats—and came to a series of steps cut into the stone wall.

She caught her breath. "Dysart, is that not a *spiral* stair?"

He glanced up from a chest he was attempting to open. "Indeed it is."

The breath she had been holding came out in a gust that set the dust motes dancing again. "Then there must be such a one in the West Tower!"

"We'll soon see, if the original plans are here." The lid to the chest came up with a blood-curdling shriek from hinges that had not moved for nearly a century. Bella crowded behind him, adding her candlelight to his as he pawed through a sheaf of yellowed parchments.

"There should be something here. I have heard that Parsifal's grandfather rebuilt the facade when he was a mere baron. Plans may have been drawn—ah, here!—no, this is an east elevation, but I trust both towers must be the same."

Bella trembled with excitement. "Dysart, we must get into the West Tower! Where is the sealed entrance? Is there not a door leading into that tower?"

"No, I looked years ago. The inside wall is closed off with stone and mortar."

She turned slowly about. "It would not have been sealed so thoroughly if there were not also a way in from the outside. There must be traces in here of the work, and if we locate them, we shall find the same on the other tower if they are alike. Do look close at the walls."

Holding his candle high, choking and coughing from the dust, Dysart began pulling aside the threadbare tapestries that covered the cold stone. "I hope you appreciate this," he remarked over his shoulder.

"Oh, but I do!"

"If there were such an entrance, it ought to be marked with stone or brick that does not match the original work, but do not hope for much."

He sounded in need of encouragement, so she supplied it. "Dysart, you are being quite wonderful."

"Indeed, I know I am, but if we find this entrance of yours, on no account am I going out in this downpour to paw through a jungle of wet shrubbery to search for—wait. Bring your candle. I think— Bella! This may be it!"

"Dysart, are you sure?" She hurried to his side. A crack in the crumbling mortar outlined an archway that could once have been a door. "Oh, Dysart, it is!"

"Damme if we haven't found it!" He caught her up in a bear-hug, spinning her about. "You have me half-believing in your theory."

"Dysart! Your candle—be careful of my hair."

"The devil with your hair. You give me hope! The Spadefield treasure may yet be found." He gave her a smacking kiss.

Bella squealed and pushed him away, patting at her endangered hair to make sure it was not afire. In the face of his excitement, she felt strangely calm, his very enthusiasm raising doubts in her contrary mind. It was too easy. Even if they broke their way into the West Tower, there might be nothing there. It had been sealed before Parsifal's time; everyone told her so.

But the spectre himself had shown her the way... or was it all her imagination?

LADY ALMERIA SEEMED very anxious to get them all upstairs and into bed that evening. The storm still howled about the house, rattling shutters and sneaking icy fingers of draft through the ill-fitting window frames. Bella caught herself wondering uneasily if there could be any truth in Dysart's tale of his grandfather's seeing Parsifal during a storm. She dismissed the idea...she thought. The earl was bamming her, hoping for a rise and a stolen kiss.

There had been no lover-like ardour in that sudden embrace. She felt more certain than ever that he had no real desire to wed her. It should be a simple matter to enlist his aid, to ask him to pretend to an affair between them to arouse Ches's jealousy. She hesitated to give false hopes to his aunts who really needed her fortune, but it could not be helped. Her whole future might depend on the subterfuge.

Safely in her bed, warmed by Mattie Ludd with bricks heated on the hearth, she pulled her quilt up over her head to block out the sounds of the storm. She tried to sleep, but her mind, like Melisande with a juicy bone, kept worrying the problem of Ches and the red-haired woman. The only solution she could see would be to waken his strong sense of chivalry and cause him to save her from the wiles of the dangerous earl. Surely, he would realize that he loved her if he believed she was about to be lost to him forever...but what if he were desperately enamoured and had formed a lasting passion for that astounding female?

She tossed for what seemed hours. Then, just as she dozed off, three ghostly knocks sounded at her door. It was after midnight. Who could it be? She tried to say "Come in," and found her voice wouldn't work. Footsteps moved away in the hall.

Propelled by a force she could not combat, she slid from her bed, stuck her feet into her slippers and went to open her door a crack.

A luminous, semi-transparent figure floated down the corridor. A short man, clad in Elizabethan velvets and wearing a long sword that dragged on the floor...she knew him at once from the portrait in the bookroom. As though wrapped in a dream, she slipped out of her room and followed him. Would he lead her to his treasure?

The bag he carried over his shoulder was empty, but as he floated along the hall, giving three ghostly raps at each bedroom door, the bag began to fill with phantom jewels and gold. He reached the great staircase and started down, his long sword bumping audibly on the steps. He tried to pull it up but it got between his legs and he stumbled. A silent, spectral curse turned the air blue about him.

Suddenly aware of what she was seeing, Bella knew a rush of pure terror and fled back to her room, losing a slipper as she ran. She fell into bed and pulled her pillow over her head. The storm outside ceased. Silence filled her chamber. Parsifal had not followed her back.

Just as she began to relax, three hollow knocks sounded again at her door. She heard it open. Footfalls crossed her floor. Frozen with horror, she huddled under the bedclothes. Was he angry because she had seen him? A horrible thought clutched at her heart. Had Parsifal come for her after all?

Driven by a desperate urgency to know, she lowered the edge of her quilt and opened one eye.

# CHAPTER NINE

ISABELLA OPENED *BOTH* eyes. She blinked in full daylight as Mattie Ludd threw back the draperies at her window with a rattle of metal rings on wooden rod.

Morning? But it could not be! It was barely past midnight! She sat up. Melisande snored at the foot of her bed. Her chamber candle had guttered out, and Mattie was carrying in her tray from the table outside her door. It *was* morning! Had she been dreaming? Or had she really seen the Old Gentleman?

Mattie discovered Melisande on the counterpane and hastily set down the tray. "Naughty dog!" she exclaimed, and picked up the indignant pug, dumping her unceremoniously on the floor. "The little mischief ran off with one of your slippers, my lady. I found it out in the hall when I came up. She had not chewed on it, fortunately, so it is not in the least damaged."

Bella tried to swallow, but her throat had gone dry. Melisande was unjustly accused. The little dog hadn't taken that slipper. She lost it in the hall herself when she fled back to bed. She *remembered* losing it.

It wasn't a dream. But how could she account for the lost time? One minute she huddled under the covers, hiding from the Spectre of Spadefield, the next, it was broad daylight. Sunshine streamed into her chamber from the window, the wind and rain had ceased, and Mattie was trying to put the bed tray of hot chocolate and buns down on her lap. Could she have fainted from sheer terror and only now awakened?

She had no appetite, but from habit she consumed two cups of chocolate and three buns.

She dressed quickly, hardly giving a grumbling Mattie time to curl her hair. The portrait of Parsifal seemed to call to her, and she hurried down to the bookroom. She must have slept late, for not only were both the Westphale ladies already there, but the sixth earl rose from his chair as she entered. Contrary to his usual bleary-eyed state, he radiated the cheer of a healthy young man who had enjoyed a good night's rest. Then Parsifal must not have appeared to him. She looked up at the portrait. Surely there was a smug cast to those painted features....

Dysart greeted her familiarly, throwing an arm about her shoulders. "Morning, luv. Ready to resume our exploration?"

Conscious of the wide-eyed stares of his aunts, she tried to shove him away, feeling the blood rush to her cheeks. "Dysart! Please!"

Lady Almeria's face glowed with an unholy joy. "Isabella! Dysart! Have you come to tell us some happy news?"

"What? Good God, no!" Dysart removed his arm as though he'd stuck it into a cauldron of boiling soup, seeming quite as shocked as Bella.

She burst into speech. "No, no. It is just that we have been... been exploring together, that is all. Dysart was showing me the old part of the house last evening."

Almeria's face fell a trifle, but she had not lost hope. "Indeed, I am excessively pleased to see you on such excellent terms. You must know, it is the wish of my heart, *both* our hearts, that you young people will grow to be the, ah, greatest of friends."

Dysart looked uncomfortable, but Bella smiled brightly, for an idea, one so fantastic that she had but barely grasped it, had sprung into her fertile mind. She caught Dysart's hand.

"Let us continue," she urged. "You must show me the rest of the west wing. I cannot have seen it all."

He eyed her suspiciously, as well he might had he known her better.

"Come along." She pinched his fingers and steered him from the room. "I must speak with you at once," she whispered in his ear.

It was not to be. As they stepped into the hall, Creswell was opening the oaken front door to a visitor. A gentleman.

For one ecstatic moment, Bella thought *Chesney! He has come!* but it was Eustace Thorpington who pushed his way past the elderly butler.

"If you please, sir," Creswell remonstrated. "I shall ascertain if my ladies are at home."

"No need, man," said Thorpington carelessly. "I can see they are."

Dysart said something under his breath that Bella, fortunately, did not understand.

"This stubbles our talk for a while," he muttered to her. "I dare not leave this cockroach alone in my halls."

Thorpington could not have failed to hear the earl's last words, spoken purposely louder, but his bland smile never wavered. "Hallo, cousin." He scarcely glanced at Dysart and turned at once to Bella. "And this must be my Lady Isabella. A beam of sunshine after our storm."

Bella disliked the man on sight. Clenching her teeth to refrain from informing him rudely that she was not *his* Lady Isabella, she extended a reluctant hand. He bent over it and to her revulsion, he pressed a wet kiss on her fingertips, bowing with a flourish if not with grace.

Dysart sneered. "What the devil do you want?"

"Why, I merely come to pay a morning call on my beloved aunts and meet their charming guest."

The charming guest surreptitiously scrubbed her damp fingers on the back of her skirt while Dysart's thundering growl echoed the storm of last night.

"They are not *your* aunts."

Thorpington shrugged. "The blood is there, several times removed perhaps, but close in my affection."

Dysart snorted like a disgusted stallion who had just breathed in a horsefly, and spun on his heel, heading back into the bookroom.

Eustace smiled at Bella. "Incorrigible youth." He shook his head, commiserating with her. "He has always been so. Quite spoiled by those sweet ladies who could never bring themselves to discipline him. We must bear with him until he grows up, for I am sure there is a sweetness within that will eventually win through."

Bella caught herself gaping at him, incredulous. Dysart was well into his twenties, a grown man, but it would have been the height of bad manners to agree that to one approaching middle age the earl might seem young. Eustace, in her eyes, must be at least thirty and five. Definitely of the older generation.

"I trust my little bouquets congratulating you upon your Presentation were to your liking?"

She tried to remember which were his and gave up. "Oh, yes. I do thank you," she managed.

He gave a self-satisfied smirk and offered his arm. Hesitating a moment, she accepted it and allowed herself to be led back into the bookroom.

The aunts, no better pleased to see Thorpington than Dysart, concealed their feelings beneath a curtain of cold courtesy. Creswell was sent for refreshments, and Bella seated herself on the hassock again, the one sure place Eustace Thorpington could not sit beside her. She listened a trifle absently to their stilted conversation, conscious of the ladies' suppressed excitement and their furtive glances at Dysart and her. The earl, luckily, only glowered at Thorpington, giving them no fuel for their suspicions. She felt a bit guilty. They did so wish for her to marry Dysart—for her fortune, of course. Remembering that, her feelings of guilt wavered.

The earl himself was an enigma, considering her wealth. Why did he not make more of a push to fix her interest? His only gallantries came when he and she were under observation by his aunts. Could it be his affections were engaged elsewhere? She recalled Mattie's tales. The abigail had definitely reported that the earl's light o' love had red hair. If it were the same woman, was Ches cutting him out? Then Dysart, if properly approached, should help her break up that affair quite willingly.

In a way, the earl's lack of desire worried her. Was she then an antidote? First Ches rejected her, then Dysart, and here was Eustace Thorpington, greed, not ardour, glowing in his shifty eyes. He had taken a chair near the doorway and kept glancing nervously at the portrait of Parsifal.

His uneasiness attracted the attention of Dysart, who bared his teeth in the smile of a wolf eying a sheep.

"Have you heard, my dear Eustace? The Old Gentleman is walking again," he murmured gently.

Bella jerked from her semi-trance, nearly upsetting the teacup Creswell had just handed her. How could Dysart know? Had Parsifal appeared to him, as well? Then she realized he only quizzed Thorpington from sheer deviltry, hoping to bring about the man's early departure. Eustace's face had blanched. What would they do, she wondered, if she told them of her experience last night?

And what of the ladies, if she mentioned that their nephew had kissed her, alone in the dark muniment room? Would that not constitute a betrothal, harmless as it was? Oddly, she had felt nothing in Dysart's embrace, whereas Ches's... She remembered Ches out on the balcony of Robisham Park in the moonlight.... Colour flooded her cheeks, and she bent quickly to tickle Terpischore's stomach. A mistake, for Melisande, ever jealous, bounded into her lap and upset the rest of her tea all over her skirts.

The incident broke up the gathering, none too soon for Thorpington, who was already on his feet. Hardly waiting to make polite farewells, he headed for the door. Lady Almeria accompanied him while Eg and Bella mopped at her drenched skirts. Almeria's voice floated back to them, her tone gently spiteful.

"Do come again soon," she told Thorpington. "And be prepared for a most interesting announcement."

Dysart cast Bella an anguished look. She smiled reassuringly over Lady Eg's shoulder, shaking her head slightly. He relaxed, but Eg's next words as Almeria returned brought him straight up in his chair.

"We've no need to worry about him." She sniffed. "I collect he's taken up with that red-haired female who owns my dog. He was leaving her house this morning when I drove by."

Dysart's eyes narrowed, and Bella subjected him to a speculative gaze. Perhaps the solution to her own dilemma would serve a double purpose. She needed to talk to Dysart, and at once.

She hastened back down to the bookroom as soon as she changed her gown. Only the ladies were still there.

"Where is Dysart?" she asked as carelessly as she could.

"He has gone out," said Lady Eg.

"For a walk round the grounds," Lady Almeria put in too quickly. "He has taken the dogs for a bit of exercise. Why do you not join him?"

Great heavens, how could she have forgotten? He must even now be searching for traces of the outside entrance to the West Tower. She glanced up at the painted Parsifal over the mantel. There—again the impression of a split-second wink.

"I do believe I shall," she said casually. "It will be quite lovely after the rain. I'll just run up and get a shawl."

"Here, my dear, take mine." Lady Almeria threw hers over Bella's shoulders and fairly pushed her towards the door. "If you hurry, you may catch him up."

*Not to worry, Godmother dear,* she thought. *I know exactly where he will be.* She accepted the shawl and went outside.

Dysart sat on the lowest step of the side terrace, staring at the base of the tower in brooding silence. He rose when she came into sight.

"I shall have to get an axe to cut away the ivy," he complained. "The blasted stuff is thick as tree limbs. And it's still wet."

Bella dropped onto the step and pulled him down beside her. "Dysart, I have a more important matter to discuss. Am I wrong in supposing your... affections to be already engaged?"

He opened his mouth, and closed it again.

"Yes, I see I am right. You do not wish to marry me any more than I do. Wish to marry you, I mean."

He nodded dumbly, and she gave him a shrewd glance.

"Then I believe our goals may coincide. Dysart, I want your assistance." She looked him over critically. "I daresay you are considered quite a prize. That is, the ladies like you?"

"What?" He sounded rather rattled.

Bella nodded firmly. "I have decided you are exactly what I need."

Now he was shaken indeed. "No! Here, now... I say... I have no wish to be caught in the parson's mousetrap!"

She tapped a foot, annoyed. "Who has said anything about marriage?"

"Didn't you?"

"Of course not!"

He wet his lips. "You must be aware of my aunt's intentions. You cannot blame me for... for being concerned."

"Believe me, marriage to you is not in my plans." She reached over and patted one of his hands.

He removed the hand and reached into his pocket for his snuff box, breathing more easily. "Then why the catechism of my charms?"

"I want you for quite another thing. How are you at seducing females?"

Dysart sneezed over his snuff and choked. "I—I beg your pardon?"

Bella's eyes widened. "I thought my question quite clear. You see, I need your help. I want you to lure that red-haired woman away from Chesney. He is the man I mean to marry, not you."

"I see." He grinned. "Oh, my aunts will not like this."

She drew herself up, folding her hands in her lap. "I am truly sorry to inconvenience them—and you—but I came to London to catch Chesney, and since my father is paying the bills for my stay, I mean to take advantage of my opportunities."

"Well, well." He leaned back, his elbows braced on the step above. "So, blows the wind in that quarter, eh?" Removing an arm, he rubbed his chin thoughtfully. "This presents an entirely new picture." He grinned at her. "What's my stake in this, luv?"

She brushed this aside. "Whatever. Your redhead, perhaps. And if we find Parsifal's fortune, you'll be able to wed where you wish."

"Even better, I'll have no need to wed at all. At least not yet."

He meant a *carte blanche*. Bella was not sure she should approve but, after all, was that not what she suspected Ches had in mind for that female?

Dysart had apparently been following the same line of thought. "I am not at all averse to your proposition, but you must know I lack the ample funds to support her in a grand style."

He agreed, however, to have a go at the widow that very evening.

ISABELLA WAS WAITING for Dysart in the library when he finally came home that night.

He had only failure to report.

"She told me she loves me," he said dismally, flopping down on the sofa next to her. "But I cannot support her as she wishes." He hesitated, glancing sideways at Bella. "She says Chesney Carlyle has the funds she seeks."

Bella had lived with a cold apprehension all evening. She felt no surprise, only the solidifying of the block of ice that had been forming inside her. She had had time to assemble a new plan in case Dysart did not succeed.

"I have decided what I must do to save him from that creature's clutches. He must be made to believe that I shall be lost to him forever if he does not turn from Mrs. Montfort and declare himself to me at once."

The earl looked at her, still despondent. "How can you be sure he will?"

"Because he loves me." Bella straightened, squaring her shoulders.

Dysart smiled crookedly. "He does?"

"He *has* to. I cannot go on otherwise. I have known him all my life, Dysart, and I believe it is his stupid pride that keeps him silent. He is a perverse snob, and thinks his rank—his *idiotic* rank!—is not equal to mine."

"He's right. There's naught you can do to change that."

"But his birth is not important to me. It is *he* that I love."

She had been able to think of only one way to awaken Ches to the fact that he could not live without her and must save her from a life of misery. Slipping her arms about the startled earl's neck, she kissed him full on the mouth.

"I accept the offer you are about to make," she told him. "We shall announce our betrothal at my come-out ball."

Pulling her arms away, Dysart scrambled to his feet. "Good God!" he exclaimed. "I am not offering for you!"

Bella smiled at him sweetly. "You shall have to. After I tell your aunts you kissed me last night in the tower room, and that we kissed again here."

His face actually paled. "You would not!"

"Odious wretch," she scolded. "One would think me a complete antidote!"

He stared at her, his eyes wide with horror.

Bella shook her head. "Oh, for heaven's sake, can you not tell when you are being hoaxed?"

"H-hoaxed?"

"Not exactly, Dysart. Only Chesney must believe us betrothed, so do not panic. As soon as he declares himself, I shall cry off."

He eyed her warily. "You will?"

"My dear gapeseed, you know perfectly well that I do not intend to marry you. It will be a *pretend* betrothal, but, Dysart, you must act the part, even before your aunts. We cannot tell anyone it is not real for fear word of our trickery will reach Chesney before he is shocked into stepping forward to save me from so tragic a mistake."

Dysart rallied. "Tragic! I like that!"

"Oh, you know what I mean. Please, Dysart. Do this little thing for me."

"Little?" The earl suddenly broke into a chuckle. "By God, I'll go along with it, if only to see Devron's face when he hears I have cut him out."

"You haven't."

"No, but he'll think it." He stopped. "Bella, do you mean to become his duchess, after all? I thought it was Carlyle for whom you set your trap."

"It is. Oh, Dysart, this must work." In her earnestness, tears sparkled on her lashes. "Chesney Carlyle is the one man in the world for me."

Dysart stretched out a hand to help her to her feet. "We'll get him for you, luv. Come, we shall tell my aunts. Lordy, but won't they be pleased! At least, for a while until they learn the truth."

Aye, there was the rub. A rush of remorse washed over Bella, and for a moment she felt quite sunk beneath it. This marriage would have meant so much to them—no, her fortune would have. She stiffened her resolve. It gave her great pain to subject them to so awful a disappointment, for she had become genuinely fond of them both, but she had to think of herself. Her future was at stake, her whole life. They would have to find another heiress, for they wanted her wealth, not her happiness.

THE AUNTS WERE ECSTATIC to learn their elusive nephew had at last been brought up to scratch. Lady Almeria terrified Bella by launching into their wedding plans.

"A formal notice must be sent to the newspapers immediately!" she cried.

"Best tell her father first," advised Eg. "He might wish to know."

"Yes, yes, of course. And posting the banns! The wedding clothes! I shall call back Madame!"

Appalled, Bella protested. "Wait. Please, wait," she begged. "I—I must have time to get accustomed to the idea. Don't tell anyone as yet. At least until after my come-out ball. I—I wish to have that one party before I am known to be committed."

Reluctantly the ladies agreed, in deference to the delicate feelings of the future bride, but no sooner were they alone than Lady Almeria turned to her sister, her eyes gleaming with triumph.

"One person at least shall hear this momentous news without delay."

Lady Eg nodded, grimly satisfied. "We must let him know his vile plans are foiled."

"You've been reading novels again," said Almeria mildly. "However, you are right."

She went to the writing desk and pulled out a sheet of paper. Finding a well-trimmed quill, she dipped it into her inkpot and began.

"My dearest Thorpington," she wrote. "It gives me the greatest pleasure to inform you..."

## CHAPTER TEN

AT BREAKFAST the next morning, kind-hearted Lady Eg noticed that Bella merely toyed with her food. She did not seem happy. Almeria, on the other hand, held forth at length on the nearing delights of Isabella's come-out, now to be a grand formal announcement ball.

"Why so formal a party?" Eg asked. "Why not let the young people have some fun? We could have a masquerade and make the announcement when they unmask."

Lady Almeria attempted to wither her with a glance and go on unimpaired, but then she looked thoughtful. Dysart hadn't been his usual cheerful self of late. He disliked formal balls, and a lavish masquerade might be just the thing to dramatize the occasion.

"I do believe you are right for once," she told Eg, waxing enthusiastic. "We shall have a masquerade, with Dysart and Bella to reign as king and queen—I must decide which ones—and we shall unmask them at midnight with a fanfare. Then will come the celebration with a triumphal spread in the drawing-rooms and free-flowing champagne for the toasts to follow. Never will London have seen a more delightful ball! Now, which royal couple should they be?"

"Louis XV and the Marquise de Pompadour," Eg suggested. "Or Henry VIII and one of his wives?"

Bella dropped a forkful of buttered egg back onto her plate. "Please, I have no desire to appear without my head."

Almeria frowned at her sister. "The first pair were not married, and as dear Isabella implies, King Henry has most disagreeable connotations. I thought more on the lines of Oberon and Titania." She sighed. "Such lovely costumes."

Eg sniffed. "Fairy wings and flowers in his hair? Dysart will have something to say about that. But dare we hold so lavish an affair after the cost of that Presentation gown?"

Almeria waved a letter Creswell had placed by her plate. "Viscount Robisham has sent me a most delightful letter. He writes that the bills from London have been pouring in and from their amounts he has deduced we are giving his beloved daughter a proper introduction to Society. He will be in raptures over this."

Anxiously, Bella broke in. "You have not told him of... of my betrothal as yet, I hope."

"You wish to tell him yourself, of course. You'd best write at once before he hears of it by way of the *Morning Post*. But your ball! Oh, dear, the invitations went out weeks ago, and if it is now to be a masquerade, all our guests must be notified of the change and at once."

"A notice in the papers?" suggested Eg.

"No, no. That would never do. Not at all the thing. Every note must be writ by hand. Good God, there will be hundreds! Eg, where is the direction of the amanuensis we hired before? Creswell, whatever do you want? Why do you stand there looking stuffed as a sausage?"

"A visitor, my lady," said the butler from the doorway to the hall. "I have placed him in the front drawing-room."

"Who? I have no time for visitors!"

"It is Mr. Carlyle, my lady."

Bella's spoon fell into her cup, splashing tea onto the tablecloth. Chesney! More than a week had gone by since he had called. Her chair scraped the floor as she pushed herself up from the table, her heart pounding.

Lady Almeria was frowning at Creswell. "Really, I cannot—" She saw Bella. "Yes. You go, my dear. He is your father's friend, and Lady Eg and I must get on with these notes."

Gratefully, Bella ran from the room. She paused in the hall, collecting herself. What should she say? Drat, she felt her cheeks flushing. She must *not* appear so eager! After all, she was about to tell him she was betrothed to another man—but how to go about it? Maybe an idea would come...

Smoothing her skirts, she patted at her curls and walked into his presence. The proper words of greeting caught in her throat as he turned from contemplation of a painting. Excessively handsome in his country attire, he always left her awestruck in his impeccable Town rig. He had dressed with care for this call, with everything prime from his romantically arranged Byronic waves to the toes of his gleaming Hessians.

He made her an elegant bow and spoke with an air of distant civility. "I hardly expected you would have time for an old friend, so taken up as you are with social engagements."

This would never do! Bella found her tongue. She reached him in two running steps and caught his hands. "Ches, I am so glad to see you. Pray forgive me, but truly my Presentation preparations filled every moment, and only wait until you hear what happened."

At her rush of words, he relaxed and became her familiar Ches. She pulled him to a sofa and sat beside him. By the time she finished the tale of her hoop being stuck in the carriage door, their old friendly relationship was well on the way to being reestablished.

"If that wasn't just like you, Izzy!" he exclaimed, just as she knew he would. "When will you grow up?"

Bella laughed, her face turned up to his...so close...she heard his breath catch and her eyes widened at the sudden warmth that darkened his. The moment passed and he moved away, placing distance between them, but elation pounded in her veins. She busied herself pleating the soft fabric of her sprig muslin skirt, trying to think of something to say that would not break the spell.

It was broken for her.

Dysart fairly bounded into the room, his usually natty attire dishevelled and his hair adorned with twigs and dead leaves. Bella and Ches both leapt guiltily to their feet.

"Guess what, luv, I have found it!" Dysart cried happily, throwing an arm about Bella's shoulders and grinning at their guest. "Hallo, Carlyle, come to join us in our treasure hunt?"

Ches made no answer. His face reddened slowly as his eyes went from Bella's blushing face to the earl's challenging expression. He bowed stiffly. "My lord."

Bella pushed Dysart away. Truly, he overacted his part! She had almost decided not to go on with their pretend betrothal, and now the nodcock had taken the matter from her hands.

Dysart, oblivious to her glare, chattered on. "It's there, just as we thought, hidden under the ivy, and the old mortar is crumbling. I believe we can break it down with ease, Carlyle, if you will lend a hand."

Ches, seeing Bella's annoyance with the rakish earl, calmed down somewhat. "Break what down?"

"We have been hunting for a way into the West Tower. Bella, here, has decided it is where the Old

Gentleman hid our family fortune. It's been bricked up for more than two centuries, and so far as is known, no one has yet searched inside it."

She joined in eagerly, anxious to explain away Ches's impression of familiarity between Dysart and herself. If what she had seen in his eyes...if it wasn't her imagination...she might have no need to shock him to his senses. "Parsifal vanishes into the western wall of the ballroom," she explained. "And it is the wall adjoining the tower. Don't you see, Ches? That must be where he guards his treasure."

Ches could only be described as sceptical. "How do you know this ghost of yours goes there?"

"Old family legends," said Dysart, giving up trying to get near Bella, who kept moving. "Everyone who has seen him reports that he goes into the ballroom."

Bella forgot herself. "I *saw* him!" she declared.

Both men looked at her in disbelief, and her chin went up. "I did. And it was *not* a dream. My slipper was in the hall where I lost it when I ran from the Old Gentleman."

The story of her dream—if it only had been a dream—came tumbling out. Ches was inclined to scoff, dismissing the slipper and blaming Melisande as had Mattie Ludd. Dysart, however, was convinced.

"Why did you not tell me of this before? We must lose no more time!" He started out, and paused. "We shall have to wait until my aunts are from home. Aunt Almeria would have a fit of the vapours if she knew we were hacking open the West Tower."

"A fit of the vapours?" Bella raised her brows. "Has she ever, to your knowledge, done so?"

"No, come to think of it. One always thinks of Aunt Eg as the tough old bird, but it was Aunt Almeria from whom I always hid when I transgressed as a child. I vow she had the second sight," he added reminiscently.

"And who has this second sight?" Lady Almeria asked from the door. "Good morning, Mr. Carlyle. Of whom do you speak, Dysart?"

The earl turned his head to smile at her. "A mutual acquaintance, known to Carlyle and myself," he said, smooth as silk. "We were telling Bella of a seance we attended."

"Faugh," said Almeria. "Footling nonsense. This ridiculous fad is spreading through the Town. I sincerely hope you will not be so deluded as to be taken in."

"Thorpington was there. Trying to contact the spirit of the Old Gentleman, if I am not mistaken. On the trail of our fortune."

Lady Almeria sniffed. "That clodpole. Much good it would do him."

Chesney stood, ready to make his departure, and Almeria held out her hand. "Must you leave so soon? But we shall see you at our ball, shall we not?" She bent towards him confidentially. "We must not say a word as yet, but I must tell you, as an old friend of Robisham's, there will be a very interesting announcement made that evening."

Such words could only have one meaning. Bella saw his face pale. He stared at her, and she stared back in dismay. Oh, drat! She had meant to call it all off! Now the matter had gone too far. She'd have to play out the scene.

Ches bowed to her curtly, said farewell to Lady Almeria, ignored Dysart and stalked from the room.

But he would come back! He *had* to come back! Surely now he would see that she must be saved from making such a misalliance and return to sweep her off her feet. In a fever of anxiety, she awaited his reaction.

CHES WALKED AWAY from Spadefield House numb with shock. One would think he had developed a tendre for the girl! Regaining his senses, he interpreted his hollow feeling of despair to fear, fear that little Bella had doomed herself to a life of misery with a profligate rake.

She must have formed a lasting passion for the handsome, glib-tongued earl. He could think of no other reason, and if Spadefield was the husband she wanted, he might as well tear up his list. Filled with noble resolve, he determined to set Dysart's feet on the straight and narrow path. He would take the errant earl under his wing and guide him away from the gaming hells and low taverns he frequented.

His first move was to run the earl to earth that evening and take him on a round of his own clubs.

With near-fatal results.

The earl was more than willing to accompany Chesney. In fact, he was in high gig and greeted him with pleasure when they met at White's that evening.

"The very man I wanted to see!" he exclaimed, pumping Ches's hand. "I have had a brilliant idea for the greatest lark! Our talk of second sight this morning brought it to my mind. We must include Fanny Montfort in our exploration of the tower!"

"Good God, why?"

"Her second sight, man. If Parsifal is there, she will sense his presence. She may even be able to contact him. We shall bring her with us and hold our own seance!" Dysart shook his head, as though marvelling that Ches could be so dense.

Ches marvelled that anyone could believe in such rubbish. He himself had the strongest doubts as to the existence of the fabled Spectre of Spadefield. He frowned, annoyed. It was his hope to divorce the widow from her spiritualist leanings, for it was all fustian. He was still determined to make Fanny respectable, and draw her into the mainstream of Society.

"Only think," Dysart continued with enthusiasm. "The Old Gentleman may yet lead us to his treasure."

Ches believed in neither the first earl nor his hoard, but he remembered the glow on Isabella's face when she spoke of Parsifal. His heart constricted. He could yet spend time in her company if he entered into their foolish game, and no one of the ton need know Fanny's part. He agreed, though yet a bit reluctantly.

"We shall have to arrange a suitable time when we can be private." Dysart scratched an ear, thoughtful. "My aunts must not know. I can not see them welcoming Fanny in the best parlour." He slapped his thigh. "Leave it all to me, I shall fix it up and arrange with Fanny. I tire of this mouldy place. Let us move on. What say you to looking in at Brooks's?"

They stepped out into the street, just as the Duke of Devron approached. Chesney paused to exchange a word with him, feeling guilty over having introduced him to Bella, knowing as he now did that the man was to be sadly disappointed when he heard the news of her betrothal to Spadefield. Almost as disappointed as he himself....

Dysart went on ahead. Ches turned away from Devron in time to see the earl's jaunty steps move him from the pool of light thrown by the flambeaux at the club's portal. As the earl walked into fog-shrouded darkness, two darker shapes loomed out of the shadows, one with a club upraised.

Shouting a warning, Ches leapt forward, catching one man by the collar and aiming a kick at the other with the club. His kick missed, but threw the assailant off balance long enough for Dysart to duck away and deflect the blow. Ches landed a wisty castor on the jaw of the man he held and another to his midsection before his captive tore free and ran. Dysart, for all his effete appearance, dealt with his attacker, wrenching away the club and flailing it at the fleeing figure.

He walked back into the pool of light, clutching his shoulder, and grinned weakly at Ches.

"I owe you my thanks," he panted. "As well as my life, I suspect."

"Hardly that."

Dysart cast him a grateful grin. "That blow, had it landed squarely, would have crushed my skull. Even glancing, it hasn't done my shoulder a bit of all right."

"Here! Are you hurt?" Ches pawed at his arm but was put away.

"Nay, man. Naught but a bruise." Dysart began to shake the arm and swing it about. "Sheer luck I ducked the way I did. Had I not turned, it might have broken the bone. As it is, the stroke slid down my arm. You know," he added, frowning, "I don't care for the odour of this. It was no street robbery, so close to the club. They meant simply to bash and run. As if they attempted a murder." He fixed Ches with an anxious eye. "Mind, not a word of this must reach my aunts."

He began to walk, and Ches fell in beside him. "Have you such an enemy? Who could want you dead?"

Dysart managed a laugh. "No one. Except, of course, old Eustace. My heir, you must know." He stopped suddenly. "By God, do you suppose..." He went on, slowly. "Aunt Almeria. She could never resist telling him he was to be cut out."

Now Ches stopped. "By your marriage?" he asked tight-lipped. "Setting up your nursery?"

"That's it."

Even though he knew the words were coming, Ches felt as if that club had struck him in the midsection, knocking out his wind. He couldn't face Dysart's company for another minute. A late hackney had stopped to deliver a passenger to his lodgings and he hailed the jarvey.

"You'd best get home and apply a poultice to that shoulder," he told the earl curtly. "Get in." He shoved him unceremoniously into the carriage.

Dysart, more shaken than he'd admit, went meekly. "Spadefield House," Ches told the driver.

He stood alone in the street, watching the carriage drive off, his mind in confusion, his senses chaotic. When had Bella ceased to be Robisham's little daughter who must be guarded and cosseted? When had she wound herself so inextricably round his heart that the thought of her lying in another man's arms bade fair to wrench that organ from his chest?

When had he fallen in love?

Unconsciously, he turned towards the one place he was sure to find comfort and solace. The night was still young, and there would be company, cards and drinks at the house on Clarges Street.

But there were not. When he was ushered into Mrs. Montfort's parlour, he found her quite alone, having called off that evening's party. She rose to welcome him with outstretched hands.

"Ah, how delightful!" she cooed. "Such a welcome change. I vow, I have been bored near to death, for I have had Mr. Thorpington to dinner and he has finally left." She drew him to a sofa, sat close beside him and began pouring out her woes, maintaining a firm hold on one of his hands.

"Mr. Thorpington," she told Chesney, "has been pressuring me for a more permanent relationship. I am facing a dire financial crisis. My mounting bills require a drastic measure and I fear I will be forced to accept a *carte blanche* from him if I am to survive."

Appalled, Chesney forgot that had been his own original idea upon first meeting the voluptuous widow. But now he knew her! She had become a friend and she could not enter a life of sin—it was not to be thought of! There must be someone willing to accept so bountifully blessed a female as a bride.

"You must remarry," he declared. "It is the only course open to you. Surely, being a wife, even of one who is yet a stranger, is far preferable."

She turned to him, clasping the hand she still clung to against her ample bosom. "But you are not a stranger." She spoke with an ardent throb in her voice. "I feel I have known you forever."

Horrified, Ches realized she thought *he* had offered for her! And he could not deny that he had spent the past few weeks virtually in her pocket. He was trapped! A man of honour did not raise expectations he did not mean to fulfil even in this female's breast!

Before he could collect his shattered wits, Mrs. Montfort threw herself upon his chest, twining her arms about his neck and holding up her face for his kiss.

What could he do?

When he managed to take his leave sometime later, he walked the streets in a daze. *He* was the green'un, not young Isabella! And what would his father say? Sir Arthur Carlyle had warned his son since early childhood against aspiring to the hand of a viscount's daughter, but what would he say to the flamboyant widow of a line officer? One who kept a gaming house? Quite a good deal, he feared.

He could see no way—no honourable way—to escape the execrable coil into which he had unwittingly plunged himself. No matter what the consequences, he was pledged to marry Fanny Montfort.

Well, and why not? The lady was not so far removed from respectability as to be an outcast, and he himself was not so high born—although the baronetcy was ancient and honourable and his father full of pride—no, he was not so high born as to require a lady of impeccable breeding for wife.

And if the fact that Bella was now lost to him forever had anything to do with his resigning himself to as tragic a misalliance as she herself contemplated, he freely admitted it.

He might as well wed the widow.

## CHAPTER ELEVEN

As THE MORNING wore on, and Chesney did not come to rescue her from the despicable Dysart and sweep her off to marry her himself, Bella fell into a fever of anxiety. Could she be so wrong about one she had known all her life? He loved her—she knew he did! Ches *must* come to her rescue. She huddled in the bookroom, in one corner of the sofa. Had she made a terrible mistake? She glanced up at the portrait above her. The painted eyes of Parsifal gazed unsympathetically into space.

Lady Almeria might be fretting like a fly in a tar barrel over the coming gala masquerade, and Isabella in a pelter over Chesney, but Lady Eglantine was concerned only with her precious Melisande, for her "time" had come. She brushed the little pug, tied a pink riband about her neck and called for the carriage. Her plans were carefully laid, and the curtain was about to rise.

Lady Almeria, passing by in her hectic rounds, noticed the preparations.

"Are you driving in the Park?" she asked. "Do take Bella with you, as she seems to be in the mopes."

Eg gaped at her sister. If she was forced to take the girl, the whole affair was ruined!

But Bella started up. "Oh, no, please. I'd rather stay at home. In...in case someone should call." And if he should not come, they might see Chesney with that...that creature—in his phaeton in the Park. Anything but that!

Both she and Lady Eg made no attempt to hide their relief when the suggestion was dropped. Fortunately for them, the inquisitive Lady Almeria had her mind on other things—the caterers, the decorators, the costumes that must be reserved. She had begun to have doubts about the fairy king and queen, and Dysart had to be consulted.

Eg made her escape. Bundling Melisande into the barouche, she directed John Coachman to drive to Clarges Street. As they turned into the little square, she saw Attila gambolling in the park, giving a flock of over-fed pigeons indigestion. The footman slept on his bench. She couldn't believe her luck. Leaning forward, she poked John Coachman in the back with the point of her parasol.

"Stop," she called, all bright and casual. "Melisande needs to stretch her legs, and if here isn't a pretty bit of garden!"

The ornamental iron gate of the minuscule park was slightly ajar, and it was the work of a moment to shove the pug through. Eagerly, Melisande began to explore this fascinating new territory, snuffling at every bush, her eyes bulging and her tiny tail aquiver.

She proceeded down the path, ever nearer the place where Attila made life miserable for the pigeons. Now, to let nature take its course.

But Lady Eg had reckoned without the popularity of this shrubby area. Attila did not romp alone. A French poodle with a regrettable trim spotted Melisande and raced over, closely followed by a miniature greyhound.

Eg pushed through the gate and shrieked for Melisande to come. She could have saved her breath. The greyhound and the poodle met and squared off, circling each other with throaty war cries. The confrontation attracted the attention of Attila, who charged up—and saw the lovely Melisande. He let out a howl of joy, and a snarling whirlwind descended on the circling pair as he threw himself into the fray.

Battle was instantly joined. Lady Eg flapped her hands helplessly. Melisande, delighted, urged the combatants on to greater gore with shrill soprano yips. The commotion roused the napping footman. Staunchly, he waded in and with a skill that spoke of long practice, he seized the poodle's collar in one hand, the greyhound's in the other and threw both dogs into the pool surrounding the fountain. Grabbing the complaining Attila, he bore him off to his end of the park.

Eg, utterly demolished, scooped up Melisande and scuttled with the protesting, struggling pug towards their carriage. Behind her, sounds of violent altercation broke out as the keepers of the poodle and the greyhound exchanged opinions with Attila's footman. John Coachman was not stupid. He whipped up his team and the horses shook the dust of Clarges Street from their hooves.

Lady Eg leaned back against the squabs and mopped her brow with the tip of her shawl, maintaining a firm grip on Melisande. Now what to do? Those men had seen her. She could never go back to that park. Would she have to contact that infamous female?

She returned to Spadefield House to find all in an uproar. Lady Almeria, pacing the bookroom floor, was countermanding directions to her harried staff, at the same time dictating the new invitations to be sent to all the guests. Two scholarly ladies from the employment office wrote as fast as they could and Bella's footmen were being sent about Town delivering them in relays.

Almeria pounced on her sister, quite overset. "Eg! The minute I saw Dysart this morning, I could tell something was wrong and I winkled the entire tale from him. He was attacked in the roadway last night and might have been killed had not Mr. Carlyle been with him! I was ready to sink!"

"Attacked?" Eg cried in consternation. "Oh, Almeria, is he badly hurt? I must go to him."

"No, no. They speedily put the rascals to rout. I have kept Dysart here this morning," she went on, looking perfectly distracted. "But I shall not be able to keep him home forever. He will not believe he is in any danger! I am sure Eustace Thorpington hired those men to attack him."

"Eustace? He would not do such a thing. He is *family*."

"Exactly. The sooner Dysart marries and sets up his nursery, the better. Do not forget, Eustace is the heir until Dysart produces another."

"Isabella," said Eg, her mind still on pups. "Bella will do the producing. Dysart will merely be the sire."

Almeria stopped pacing, shocked. "Eg, how can you be so vulgar? Suppose sweet, innocent Isabella were sitting right here!"

BELLA WAS NOT SITTING there because she was outside by the base of the West Tower, inspecting the bricked-up doorway Dysart had uncovered.

The sixth earl came bounding round the corner from the bookroom terrace, his golden curls tousled as though he'd run his hands through them repeatedly.

"Have you heard what my aunt is planning?" he shouted as he came. "Oberon and Titania! We should look utter fools!" He calmed down a trifle when he reached her side. "I'm not dressing up in wings and flowers in my hair as some demmed—pardon me—fairy! If they must have *A Midsummer Night's Dream,* I shall go as Bottom and wear an ass's head. Far more appropriate, in the circumstances."

"You are not regretting our game?" she asked, anxious. "It is now too late to back out."

"No, no. I'll play along." He grinned. "Rather fun, getting such a rise from Carlyle."

"Oh, Dysart, do you really think so?"

"Can you doubt it? When I mentioned starting my—that is, getting wed, I thought he'd finish the job those thugs had begun. Well, I mean, he looked ready for murder."

Bella had read in novels of heroines whose hearts sang. She had never believed it until this moment. Her heart—nay, her whole soul—was singing. "Then he will come!" she cried.

Dysart looked at her perplexed. "Of course he will come. He is to bring Mrs. Montfort to hold a seance in the tower for us."

A seance? Bella descended to earth with a thump. Chesney had attended a seance, and it was at the home of that red-haired female. And now he would bring her *here!*

Dysart had cheered considerably. "She has the 'sight,' you must know, and will it not be the greatest rig if she can contact the Old Gentleman?"

Bella turned and walked back to the terrace, her lips tight. "Do you really think that wise?"

"Certainly! Why, even Eustace thought Parsifal might reveal his secret." He trotted to keep up with her. "We want to find his loot, if he did not gamble it all away on the Continent, do we not? If Fanny Montfort can conjure up his spirit we might at last learn the answer."

She reached the French doors to the front drawing-room and he followed her inside.

"We must have Fanny. Only think what a lark, a seance at midnight in a haunted tower."

Bella stopped in the middle of the drawing-room carpet. "M-midnight?"

"Naturally. All seances are conducted at midnight. It seems to be one of the rules."

As he spoke, a series of hollow, bumping sounds came from the hall. For a moment, they both froze. But it was broad daylight! No self-respecting spectre walked before midnight! Dysart pushed past Bella, who hung onto his arm and was dragged willy-nilly into the hall.

The thumps came from the curving staircase, but it was not Parsifal who descended. Melisande rounded the landing, dragging after her one of Dysart's boots.

The earl exploded. "My new white-tops! I'll kill the little beast if she's chewed them!"

Melisande, who knew that bellow of old, dropped the boot and stood not upon the order of her going. She galloped back up the stairs, and Dysart ran to retrieve his property. He came back down, examining his precious boot and muttering.

"She's forever carrying off our footwear. This time she's done no damage, thank God, but I shall not leave my chamber door open again."

Bella leaned against the newell post, letting out a long sigh of relief. It was followed by an indrawn gasp of realization. Her sighting of Parsifal *could* have been a dream! It must have been. Chesney was right, as he always was, and it was Melisande who had taken her slipper out into the hall. She had only dreamt that she'd lost it.

"I say, Bella," Dysart remarked, "we'd best do our treasure hunt this very night if I can arrange it with Fanny. Once you come out, you'll not have a moment free."

"But I am to go to a soirée this evening. Your aunts have been most insistent, for it is given by one of their dearest friends."

"Nothing could be better. You must develop the headache and they will go without you. I'd best be off for Fanny's at once to set all up."

Bella retired to the bookroom to await his return, taking a hand in the writing of the new addition to the invitations alongside several harried secretaries. An hour passed before Dysart appeared in the doorway. His face was pale beneath his shock of light hair. He motioned across the frenetic activity in the room for her to join him. In the hall, he clutched her arms.

"Bella, he has offered for her! Fanny is going to *marry* Carlyle!"

BELLA HAD NO DIFFICULTY at all simulating a headache. Indeed, she had one, and a sick heart, as well. How could Chesney have done such a thing? And how could she have been so nit-witted as to drive him to it? For driven she was convinced he was, and not only by herself. That red-haired woman had seduced him expertly into a lush and fragrant trap and slammed the boudoir door behind him before he knew what had happened. Never, never would he marry beneath him, for that pride of his worked both ways. He had been treading a narrow path, ever surefooted, until she—like a fool!—pushed him from it.

And poor Dysart! From the look on his face when he gave her the calamitous news, he was as *bouleversé* as she. She had suspected the earl's heart to be given elsewhere, but never had she thought Ches would offer for the woman Dysart loved. A *carte blanche*, perhaps, but *marry* her? Oh, this was all her fault!

Four lives would be ruined because of her stupidity. Well, three at any rate, hers, Ches's and Dysart's. The Widow Montfort was no doubt *aux anges*, about to wed the handsomest man in London—in Bella's opinion—and one of the richest. Even if the widow loved Dysart as he obviously did her, Mrs. Montfort would never cry off this engagement, not with the Carlyle fortune so nearly in her hands.

THE HOUR FOR DEPARTURE came, and John Coachman drew up in front of Spadefield House. With many wishes for Bella's improvement and adjurations for her to go to bed immediately with a *tisane* for her head, Lady Almeria and Lady Eg left for the soirée without her. The carriage was hardly out of sight before Chesney swung his curricle into the stable yard. Fanny Montfort sat beside him—and on her lap sat Attila.

"Confound it!" exclaimed Dysart. "Why the devil did you bring the dog?"

Ches was handing the widow down from the two-wheeled carriage, and she waited until she stood on solid ground before answering.

"Animals can tell," she informed him, hugging her pug. "If a spirit is near, he will know."

"Keep a tight hold on the little beast," Dysart growled. "My aunt's Melisande is 'that way.' If he gets loose we may be up to our, ah, elbows in pug puppies. Well, come along, dog and all. I've found the bricked-up entrance hidden under a mass of ivy we'll have to chop away."

Bella had been standing aside, and Chesney, ever conscious of his manners, led Mrs. Montfort up to her. The widow cheerfully failed to recognize the icy manner in which she, being every inch the Lady Isabella, acknowledged the introduction. The way that...that *woman* clung to Chesney's arm! Resentfully, Bella noted the widow's possessiveness and her continual smiles up at him as they all followed

Dysart around to the tower. Surely, whatever that female had to say to Chesney could be said aloud. There could be no need to constantly whisper for his ears alone.

Dysart had raided the garden shed for picks and hatchets. Bella was forced to wait beside Mrs. Montfort while Ches and Dysart, with a bit of quiet cursing, hacked a way through the ivy. The widow was redolent with some musky scent that Bella found nauseating. How could that pug in her arms stand it? Animals had such sensitive noses.

"How can you wear such strong scent around your little dog?" she asked coldly. "I am sure the Westphale ladies' pugs could not bear to be near it."

Fanny Montfort gave clear evidence that she recognized an enemy when she met one. "Males prefer my perfume," she replied sweetly. And that was the extent of their conversation. Widow, one. Bella, naught.

The men made short work of clearing away the worst of the ivy and now tackled the exposed brick. After much labour and more cursing, helped by the crumbling of the centuries-old mortar, they managed to make a hole large enough to crawl through. Dysart had brought a lantern and Ches knelt to strike it alight. The sudden flare startled Attila, and Mrs. Montfort, bending to watch, failed to grip the dog firmly.

Dysart let out a shout as Attila leapt to the ground and ran in circles around them, barking.

"Catch him!" he yelled, chasing after the pug.

Delighted with the game, Attila ran in wider circles and Fanny clapped her hands, shouting encouragement—to the earl, not Attila, but it had a reverse effect. Dysart nearly caught him once, but the pug wriggled free and took off across the lawn, both the earl and the widow in hot pursuit.

Chesney, uninterested, climbed through the hole they had made, taking the lantern. Bella couldn't wait to see if there would be a spiral staircase inside. She hitched up her skirts and followed him.

He moved the light around the musty, damp stone room and set it down on a flight of steps. Spiral steps, disappearing up and up into the palpable blackness above. Parsifal had not failed her! Eagerly, Bella ran ahead, starting to climb.

Ches stopped her, catching her skirt and pulling her back. "You're not going up there yet! Wait for me down here until I am sure all is safe."

Taking the lantern, he began to work his way up the steep stairs, steadying himself with one hand against the stone of the wall. The light he carried moved up with him, leaving her in utter darkness. She waited, hugging herself against the chill of nerves and anticipation. Unbidden thoughts of spiders and rats crept into her mind. Quite willing to let him clear away the cobwebs and frighten any vermin who might have nests above, she started to climb back outside. Voices approached. Dysart and Mrs. Montfort had caught Attila and were coming back to the tower. Believing themselves alone outside, they talked.

"I cannot afford to whistle such a fortune down the wind," Mrs. Montfort was saying. "I must wed Mr. Carlyle, but I see no reason for my marriage to interfere with our pleasant arrangement. But give me a few weeks to settle in, and I shall be delighted to receive a visit from you."

Dysart sounded profoundly shocked. "Fan, I could not! One does not have an affair with the wife of a friend. It is not at all the thing!"

Bella shrank back, spiders and rats forgotten. She must tell Chesney at once! But what if he truly loved this calculating female? Oh, he could not! Not after hearing this!

She became aware of Chesney behind her, holding the lantern to light her way to the steps.

"Come on up—there is only a bare room at the top of the stairs with enough moonlight through the arrow-slits on the outside walls so we can see. Where are Dysart and Mrs. Montfort?"

Desperately concerned with what she had overheard, Bella hurried up to him, anxious to speak before they were joined by the others.

"Ches, that woman does not love you—she weds you only for your fortune! You must cry off!"

He turned on her, as shocked as Dysart had sounded in response to Fanny's suggestion. "Bella, you know I cannot!"

"But I heard her, Ches. She told Dysart so, just now." Bella could not bring herself to tell *all* she had heard.

The light from the lantern illumined his face and she saw him frown unhappily. "Indeed, I know that is true, but, Izzy, once a gentleman is known to have made an offer, he is committed, bound by the code of honour. If I do not go through with this marriage, I can never hold up my head again."

"Drat your head!" she exclaimed. "How can you let a silly thing like honour stand in your way when you know she has none?"

Chesney, pinked fairly in his most vulnerable tenet, drew himself up. "Honour," he declared, "is the one law for which an English gentleman will lay down his life."

*Men!* "Oh, bother your honour!"

"Hush, now. Here they are."

There came sounds of a difficult entry. Dysart was apparently attempting to boost in the buxom widow with one arm while clutching the struggling Attila under his other.

"Bring over that demmed—pardon me—light," he panted. "Or help me with this dog!"

To Bella's fury, Ches set down the lantern and took the widow, not the dog, placing his hands about her waist and pulling her through the hole they had made. She came, full of girlish squeals and somehow managing to get her arms about his neck. Tipping up her face, she coyly invited him to kiss her, but Ches set her firmly on the ground.

Dysart picked up the lantern and swung it about the bare room in which they stood. Small dark creatures scuttled away over the hard-packed earth floor, pursued by Attila. White crawly things retreated from the light, creeping into cracks in the stone of the walls. Fanny Montfort's squeals became genuine.

"Why don't you wait outside?" Ches suggested.

"No, indeed!" she exclaimed. "And miss a real spectre? But do keep that lantern near my feet. I shall feel quite safe if I have your arm about me."

"Well, you can't have it," Dysart put in disagreeably. "These steps are only wide enough for one at a time. Come on, Carlyle, go first with the lantern and hold it so we can all see where we're putting our feet. You ladies go next and I'll bring up the rear to catch you as you fall."

To Bella's disgust, Mrs. Montfort squealed again and seized Ches's coattails, nearly pulling him from the steps. She herself disdained Dysart's assistance and carefully followed the widow, one hand tracing the wall to keep her balance as she mounted the narrow, slippery steps. Even the stones of the wall were slimy with damp and mould.

Dysart cursed suddenly and almost lost his footing. The next moment, a solid wriggling little body forced itself between Bella's feet, and she would have fallen had Dysart not steadied her. Then Mrs. Montfort shrieked and threw her arms about Ches's waist. He clung to the lantern somehow and swore. Free at last of the slow-moving humans, Attila bounded up the steps ahead of them.

The tower, Bella knew from seeing the outside, was four storeys tall. Then why did the steps go on for at least a mile? Round and round she went, hugging the cold wall beside her closer and closer as they rose. She thanked the powers that be for the darkness that had terrified her at first; at least it hid all below her so she could not see how high they had come. She now clutched the skirts of the woman above her with her free hand and was grateful for the light pressure of Dysart's fingers on her waist. Then, hours after beginning their climb—or was it only interminable minutes?—she saw pale light issue from above.

"Moon," said the earl. "There are windows at the top."

The room they finally reached was completely empty in the glow from their lantern. Ches turned the light slowly, swinging it round the walls and floor. Nothing in the way of a treasure chest, that was certain, nor was there a niche or alcove. The only openings were the narrow slits that had served as arrow-loops for the bygone archers. Nevertheless, they searched every inch of the timbered floor and as far up the stone walls as they could reach, finding nothing but dust, cobwebs and a few ancient bird nests.

Attila, who joined in, snuffling along the base of the wall, suddenly stopped and began to whine at an empty corner, wagging his curly tail.

"He is here!" intoned the widow, closing her eyes and shielding them with one hand while she held the other, fingers outstretched, before her. "Attila has sensed a presence from the grave."

"Actually," said Dysart, "we are not sure the Old Gentleman was ever placed in a grave."

Mrs. Montfort opened her eyes. "He must have been."

Attila stopped whining and sat down, awkwardly scratching his ear with a short hind leg. His mistress eyed him fondly. "At any rate, Parsifal's ghost must be here. Animals are sensitives, you know."

"So I imagine," agreed Ches. "I expect he has sensed a rat."

She ignored the unbeliever and turned to Dysart, speaking once more in her sepulchral seance voice. "Let us try to contact your spectre."

An eerie, pervasive coldness filled the shadowed room. Bella shivered. "Let us not. Not in here."

Even Dysart was looking over his shoulder uneasily. "The Old Gentleman only walks during the full moon," he said, as though convincing himself. "He wouldn't be here now."

The widow was agreeable. "Then we shall hold our seance in this tower when the moon has reached the full."

For all that she claimed not to fear the wraith of Parsifal, Bella had a sudden urge to leave. The very shadows beyond the lantern's pool of light seemed to float and waver. "Yes," she said, refusing to let her voice quaver. "Some other time. Let us get down from here."

There were no dissenters, excepting possibly Attila who was inclined to continue his rat hunting. They descended carefully, and Bella did not draw a full breath until she clambered through the hole and out into the fresh night air.

Ches went at once to retrieve his curricle. Bella, with Dysart beside her, watched him hoist his loathsome widow and the pug Attila onto the seat and drive off. She and the earl went back into Spadefield House by the drawing-room French doors, which Dysart had left unbolted.

He glanced at her woebegone face. "I could do with a libation. How about you?"

She nodded listlessly and sank down on a sofa. A few minutes later he returned, and she accepted the wine he brought her.

"Dysart," she began, hesitant, "I have come to a decision. We should pretend to be betrothed no longer."

Collapsing into an armchair, he sipped from his portion of brandy. "Hasn't worked out all that well, has it?"

"I mean, I've decided to really marry you."

He sat up. "Here, now! I protest!"

"What else is there for us to do?" She spread her hands. "Ches is determined to wed his . . . his widow and I cannot see her letting him go. She is as lost to you as he is to me."

Dysart cupped his hands about his glass and looked at her for a long minute. "I suppose...I shall have to marry someday and I guess you will do as well as another."

"Thank you."

His generally devilish grin went sadly awry. "All right. Better than most. You don't have fits of the vapours or take confounded freaks, and the Old Gentleman seems to like you. It will not be easy, but I shall try to survive."

Bella picked up a pillow and threw it at him. He caught it with a weak attempt at a laugh.

"Yes, that is what I mean. We should deal tolerably well." He rose, holding out his hands. "Come here, then."

She realized he meant to kiss her to seal their bargain, and went to him. It should have been exciting to be kissed by so personable a gentleman, but he might as well have been a brother, so casual a salute it seemed. No bells rang, no fireworks went off, she felt no need to swoon like the heroine of a gothick novel. This first caress presaged no thrills in their coming marriage.

BELLA WENT UP TO BED, but not to sleep. For hours, she lay awake, heartsick over Ches's idiotic blindness to all but his honour.

Her attention was caught by a sound from the hall outside her chamber. A footstep? It came again—and again. Someone, or *something* walked past her door. Her thoughts leapt at once to the Spectre of Spadefield. Had they roused him by invading his tower?

Sticking her feet into her slippers, securely this time, she crept to her door and opened it a crack.

A candle on one of the wall sconces had escaped snuffing and had not quite guttered out. In its flickering light, a shadowed figure moved down the hall—a short man, dressed like the portrait above the bookroom mantel, in hose and doublet and sporting an Elizabethan neck-ruff... Parsifal! To be sure she was not dreaming, she gave her arm a sharp pinch and it hurt.

But something was wrong. This ghost carried no sack, nor did he glow. Curiosity won out. Her heart pounding, she eased through her door and followed silently down the corridor. No doors were knocked upon. The dark figure went straight to Dysart's bedchamber.

She tiptoed to the door and peeked in. Pale moonlight from an undraped window lit a horrifying scene. The too-substantial ghost had pulled the counterpane from over Dysart and was smothering him with it.

Bella looked about wildly for a weapon. She rushed in, caught up Dysart's dressing-table stool and smashed it down on the "phantom's" skull. He staggered, holding his head, and nearly fell. Bella grabbed at his doublet as he dashed from the room. He jerked away and she felt the fabric tear. She was knocked against the doorframe as he escaped. Clutching her own head, she sank to her knees.

The man had fled before Dysart regained his senses enough to fight free of the counterpane. Bella heard footsteps pounding along the corridor, and ran to him.

"Quick, Dysart! He's getting away!" She tore at the bedclothes, yanking both them and the dazed earl onto the floor. "He went that way!"

Dysart shoved her aside, and she was slammed into the doorframe again as he careened groggily out into the hall.

Melisande, aroused by the racket, chased the invader, yapping with delight, and Terpsichore puffed and panted in her wake. Dysart fell over the elderly pug, sprawling his length on the hall carpet. Their quarry raced down the staircase and into the pitch-dark ballroom on the floor below.

The sound of heavy footfalls ceased.

Bella and Dysart reached the ballroom together and stopped, listening. Complete silence. They were alone.

But not for long. The two younger footmen, in varying degrees of undress, bounded up the stairs from the servants' quarters below. They were followed by Creswell in purple flowered dressing gown, nightcap and Turkish slippers, a startling apparition in the glow from the candlestick he carried. The footmen crowded up behind this bulwark of safety and peered around it.

The butler held his candle high. The ballroom was empty. Like the ghost of Parsifal, the would-be murderer had simply disappeared.

## CHAPTER TWELVE

"MY LORD," Creswell asked, a quaver in his voice. "What is happening?"

"Not a thing," Dysart replied, managing to sound nonchalant. "A false alarm. Lady Isabella fancied the Old Gentleman was passing her door and gave chase, wakening me on the way."

Creswell seemed doubtful. "Running I heard, my lord. Was that you?"

"We both ran, hoping to get a glimpse of our spectre, but luck was not with us."

Bella started to speak, but Dysart signalled her to silence.

"Not one word of this to my aunts, if you value your positions," he told the butler and footmen. "I'll not have them frightened. Go back to bed." Bella pulled at his sleeve, shaking her head, and he glanced down at her pale face. "On second thought, why don't you three keep watch here tonight? There's always a chance Lady Isabella might be right," he added, bland as blancmange.

This did not go over well with the domestics, who moved closer together, peering into the shadows nervously.

Dysart gave them a gentle smile. "Best get a few more candles." The dogs were snuffling about in the darkness, and he called them to heel. They ignored him. He shrugged and pressed Bella's cold fingers. "Up we go, my lady. You couldn't be in safer hands." They left the pugs to keep Creswell and his minions company.

When they reached the bedroom corridor, both Lady Almeria and Lady Eglantine were peeking out their doors, their heads adorned with lace-trimmed nightcaps.

"What is going on?" Lady Almeria demanded.

Dysart gave an exaggerated sigh. "Can't keep a thing from you two needle-wits. Nothing to worry you, luvs. Bella heard noises downstairs and hoped it was the Old Gentleman, so she roused the house. It was an old gentleman, all right, but only Creswell checking to make sure he'd cast all the bolts."

"It couldn't have been Parsifal," Lady Eg told Bella kindly. "The moon is not yet full."

Bella felt Dysart press her hand urgently. She forced a bright smile. "I do apologize. I have been quite silly, and far too fanciful."

Dysart patted her shoulder. "No harm done. Good night, all."

The aunts' doors closed and Dysart began to massage a turned ankle incurred during his fall over Terpsichore. They were standing beneath the guttering wall sconce, and as he bent, he caught sight of Bella's face and left off his ministrations to himself.

He stared at her. Her hand went up to a swelling bruise on her forehead and cheekbone where she had struck her head on the doorframe in his room.

Dysart grinned. "You'll have a black eye in the morning, luv."

OTHER THAN A BROKEN LEG on Dysart's dressing-table stool, his turned ankle and Bella's blackened eye, they sustained no serious damage in the attack of the previous evening. Creswell and the two footmen might have disagreed, having spent a sleepless night, but their opinions were not solicited.

It had begun to rain again, a heavy overcast sky obscuring the sun. The depressing weather quite suited Bella's mood as she left her room that morning. She encountered the sixth earl in the corridor.

"One good thing," he told her. "No one will notice our hole in the tower. Who'd be addlepated enough to venture out in this downpour?"

"Certainly not me. At least, not looking like this."

He peered at her in the gloom of the hall. "My, my. You do resemble one of the Fancy who has lost a match."

It was not a flattering simile, and she glared at him. "It's your fault. You knocked me into the door."

"Not the first time. You told me my would-be assassin did the thing when he ran out."

"Yes, but it didn't help a second time." She touched her eyebrow and cheekbone gingerly. "It hurts."

Instantly he dropped his teasing manner. "Poor Bella. I am sorry to be the cause of your pain." Before she knew what he was about, he tipped up her face and kissed her gently on the injured brow. "All my wretched doing."

"Yours!"

"Aye. If I had attended to my duty and married years ago, this never would have happened. It was Eustace, I suspect, or someone he hired. He is determined not to be cut out of the inheritance. He wants the Old Gentleman's loot, and he intends to get his hands on Spadefield House by any means he can."

"Surely Parsifal will not let him! Oh, dear heavens, do you suppose he got in through our hole in the tower?"

The earl concentrated for a moment. "No, I saw no way into the house from there—other than the ground-floor entrance, but that is still bricked up and panelled over on the drawing-room side. And he did not leave that way. He vanished in the ballroom."

"Then that is where we must search!"

"Yes." Dysart remained thoughtful. "It almost looks as though Eustace—if it is he—has some reason to be convinced the Old Gentleman's fortune is still here. That being the case, if it exists we'd best find it, if only to send Eustace packing before I am removed from his path."

"Oh, no! That must not be. Can we not call in the Watch or something? We cannot let him get away with trying to kill you." Distressed, she caught his hand to her cheek.

Dysart shook his head. "I have no proof that it is Eustace." He pressed a kiss into her palm. "I can, however, marry as soon as possible and when there is a direct heir, I trust he will give up."

"But that will take time! How can we keep you safe until then?"

"I do appreciate your solicitude." He grinned, caught her in his arms and kissed her again.

"Dysart!"

"Get used to it, luv. I quite like kissing you." He let her go suddenly. "Oh, the devil. If only we were free of this coil." He turned and strode away leaving her standing alone in the corridor.

She knew how he felt, for she was aware of it, too—the return of that sense of desolation when both were reminded of the reason for their coming marriage. *Chesney, how could you?* She walked slowly down to the breakfast room.

Lady Almeria, in a stew over the masquerade, was speaking as Bella entered.

"Dysart refuses to be Oberon. Now I shall have to order new costumes and we are behind all our guests! All the best rigs will be reserved. I did so want them to dress as a pair of great lovers of history, such as Romeo and Juliet, but there may be no costumes left."

"Adam and Eve?" suggested Lady Eg.

"Really!" exclaimed her sister. "Do be serious. Ah, there you are, Isabella. Which costume would you prefer?"

"Anything you wish." Bella sank into a chair and gazed at the empty plate before her. How could she be expected to celebrate what to her was a tragedy? Depicting herself and Dysart as famous lovers was laughable, only she could not laugh. She probably never would again.

At this point, Lady Almeria happened to glance at Bella. She rose slowly from her chair. "Great heavens! What has happened to you?"

"Really, it is nothing," Bella explained hastily. "I merely ran into a door last night in the dark."

"But look at her!" Almeria wailed to Eg. "What are we to do? She cannot appear in public like this! We must cancel all our engagements."

Lady Eg eyed Bella with interest. "She is rather colourful, is she not? What excuse shall we give? Measles?"

"Why not tell the truth?" Bella suggested, not caring. "Say I cannot go out because I have a blackened eye."

"Do not be a goosecap." Lady Almeria spoke sharply. "You are merely indisposed." She rose to inspect Bella more closely. "I hope to goodness that will fade before we must make our great announcement."

"Yes," Eg agreed. "It would not be at all the thing for your face to be purple and green."

"With luck, the colour may go with my costume." Bella tried to smile. "After all, it is a masquerade. Perhaps I could keep my mask on."

"No, no. You are both to unmask at midnight," Lady Almeria decreed. "I have planned such a lovely pageant. First, the hired waiters will circulate among the guests with glasses of champagne, then there will be a fanfare from the musicians to gather everyone's attention. You and Dysart will be standing between the double doors. Thomas and Henry, in their lavish Robisham livery, will advance, clearing a path for our royal couple as you walk the length of the room."

It sounded much like her Presentation and Bella opened her mouth to protest. She did not have a chance. Lady Almeria sailed on, becoming enthusiastic.

"I have planned for the musicians to be at the back of the ballroom so everyone will get an excellent view of you. When you reach them, they will play another fanfare. I shall step up between you and make the announcement." Here, she strode forward a few steps, raised her arms and declaimed, "I give you Dysart, sixth Earl of Spadefield and his bride-to-be, Lady Isabella Greenlea of Robisham Park!" She stepped back. "Then you will both unmask and bow, to the applause of our guests and the drinking of a toast."

"Shouldn't the lady's name go first?" asked Eg.

Lady Almeria waved this aside impatiently, "I daresay. A small detail to be ironed out later."

Eg was still puzzled. "How will they applaud while holding glasses of champagne?"

Thoroughly annoyed, Lady Almeria turned on her sister, prepared to deliver a verbal onslaught. Lady Eg was saved by the appearance of Creswell.

"Mr. Chesney Carlyle, my ladies," he announced. "Are you at home?"

Bella sprang up before she thought.

"Yes, do you see to him, Isabella." Lady Almeria pushed her towards the door. "He'll not mind your eye. No doubt he has heard our news somehow and has come to wish you happy."

Or to beg her to cry off. Hope buoyed her into the hall, her feet scarcely touching the floor. Then she remembered Ches's own betrothal, and paused. He hadn't yet seen her. Creswell was divesting him of his many-caped greatcoat, letting it drip on the stone-flagged floor, while Ches shook the water from his curly-brimmed beaver. His dark hair was set with raindrop diamonds, sparkling on the lock that always escaped and lodged over his brow. As ever, Bella's breath caught in her throat at the sight of Mr. Chesney Carlyle. Her every nerve awoke, aware of his physical attraction.

Creswell was not a small man, but Ches topped him by half a head. He was much the same height as Dysart, she realized, but oh, such a difference! Ches was dark and romantic-looking as Byron but every inch a Corinthian, honourable, dependable, faithful—unfortunately to the wrong woman. Dysart was Viking blond, as handsome as Ches in his own way, a dangerous rake—and the man she had promised to marry. Was there ever such a coil?

Lady Almeria's voice carried out into the hall. "Very well, Eg," she was saying. "We shall dispense with the applause. I shall call out 'A toast, a toast!' and that will fix all."

At her words, Ches looked up and saw Bella. His face lit up, and faded as he must have remembered how matters stood.

Forgetting her bruised face, Bella ran to greet him. He stared at her, aghast.

"Bella! What has happened to you?"

Her hand went to her bruise. "Does it look so awful? I expect it must have been when Dysart knocked me into the doorframe."

*"What!"* His thunderous expression scared her.

"Not on purpose," she amended hurriedly. "It was an accident. I was saving his life."

"Bella." His tone was so stern that she shrank back. "Bella, tell me all, with none of your roundaboutation."

"Yes, of course, but not here." She led him away from the disappointed butler, into the front drawing-room. Beginning with the footsteps passing her door, she recounted the attack on Dysart and her part in driving off the would-be murderer.

Chesney was first appalled, then furious. "How could you take such a chance? Izzy, if that is not just like you! You do not think." He gripped her shoulders and shook her. "Good God, you little idiot, you might have been killed!"

Bella, whose mind had been occupied with him and his widow all night, struck back. "A l-lot you would c-care!"

"Care!" He still gripped her shoulders and suddenly his arms went about her, crushing her in a desperate embrace. "Care—I could not live in a world without you. Bella, I love you so much—" He heard his own words and the blood drained from his face. "Good God, I should not have said that. I have kept silence for all these years. Oh, hell—"

His iron control broke. The force of his embrace lifted her from the floor, and she clung to him, returning the kisses he pressed on her eyes, her cheeks, her lips. If this was all they were to have, she made the most of it, torn between the heaven of the moment and despair that it was the end. Her arms were about his neck and he nuzzled his face in her hair, whispering the words she had longed forever to hear. He held her as though he could never let her go.

"How can I live without you?" he murmured in a ragged voice that caught, suspiciously like a sob. "It near as naught drives me to Bedlam to see him lay a hand on you. What will happen to me when you are wed? When I think of you in his bed—Bella, I shall have to leave the country to keep from murdering him."

At this she pulled back enough to speak. "Then why have you been such a idiot? But for your foolish honour... if only you had told me you loved me, I need not have pretended to be betrothed to Dysart."

"Pre-pretended?"

"Yes, to make you realize you loved me."

He held her away, his hands on her shoulders, shaking her again in helpless fury. "If that isn't just like you! To pretend! And plunge us all into this bumble-broth! I ought to box your ears!"

"It's all your fault!" she retaliated. "You and that red-haired female. And... and you would have seen me wed to the Duke of Devron before you came to your senses!"

"I only thought—at least, *then* I thought—you would be safe with him, taken care of."

She was shaking by herself now, shaking with mounting wrath. "How could you have thought that pop-eyed caricature of Prinny a suitable husband for me?"

"He had all the qualifications."

"What qualifications? For what?"

Ches hesitated, taken aback. "For a husband. You see, when you told me you were coming to London to get married, I thought I'd best—that is, I made a list—see here, Bella, you cannot just marry anyone. The man must measure up."

"To what?" she demanded, her lips thinned.

In desperation, he dragged a dog-eared scrap of paper from his pocket. "After that night at Robisham Park, I thought of all the things a man must have to be worthy of you and I wrote them down. You see, I do not qualify at all, failing rank at once, but Devron—"

She held out her hand. "Give me that list." She snatched it from him and read it over. "Rank—wealth—consequence—you might as well throw this away, Ches." She shook her head at him slowly. "You have left off the only one that matters, the one qualification that outweighs all the rest."

"I've felt there was something missing, but I couldn't think what it was."

"The man must love me, Ches. Me. Not my money or my pretty face. Me."

For that point, Ches realized, he was overqualified. But what could he do? "Bella, I cannot back out of my commitment. I am sure Fanny has spread it all over Town. I must marry her or be labelled a cad, a bounder, a skirter. You may cry off, however. There is no hold on you."

"Is there not?" she wailed. "Oh, Ches, if I cannot marry you, I do not care who the man may be. I'd best take Dysart. His aunts are counting on my fortune to save their beloved Spadefield House. I cannot have them thrown out into the streets, or worse, into the poorhouse."

It was a tragic impasse. In all conscience, they must part forever. Bella held up her face for one last kiss. But even this they were not to have.

Lady Almeria's raised voice sounded from the bookroom. "Indeed? We shall see. I shall ask Isabella's opinion at once!"

Pushing Chesney away, Bella ran for her room. Tears streamed down her cheeks, for she knew that what she had felt for Chesney before had been a mere childish infatuation. Only now did she know the incredible pain and glory of true love.

That night she sat long at her window, watching a drizzle of rain that matched her mood. The dark sky began to clear and through fitful clouds she glimpsed a waxing moon. In their excitement over Dysart's betrothal to Bella and the changing of their ball to a masquerade, the aunts had miscalculated.

It was quite likely there would be a full moon on the night of the ball. Bella was too miserable to care.

## CHAPTER THIRTEEN

A WEEK PASSED without sight of Chesney Carlyle, and it was the night of Bella's gala come-out ball. Her eye had faded enough to be almost disguised by a heavy layer of rice powder that she knew would have to be hastily redone when she removed her mask. She stood now at the entrance to the ballroom, between the two Westphale ladies, waiting to greet their guests.

In decorating the room, Lady Almeria had tried to recreate the days of the first earl, and the result was truly spectacular. Or at least, Bella amended, it was a true spectacle. If her father judged her social success by the amounts of the bills he received, he should be ecstatic.

Ancient gonfalons, threadbare tapestries and rusting shields resurrected from the storage rooms hung on the walls. Hundreds of candles blazed from the three chandeliers, and tapers flamed in the wall sconces, no doubt representing medieval torches. Garlands of green paper leaves, studded with pink silk flowers, streamed from the base of the central lustre. From there they were swagged to meet the tops of eight-foot potted palms where the garlands ended in a flourish of ruffles and ribbon bows. The palms, placed at intervals along the sides of the great room were flanked by rusting suits of armour, each holding baskets of real flowers. The air was redolent with the fragrance of the blooms and the scent of burning beeswax. Lady Almeria had created a fantasy land, and Bella was certain neither Parsifal—nor anyone else—had ever seen its like.

The string quartet hired to play for the dancers began to tune their instruments, and she could hear guests arriving in the hall below. Taking a deep breath, she adjusted her loo-mask and prepared to be polite. The next hour passed in a blur of masked faces and names she forgot as soon as they were announced. One name stood out by its absence. She had not seen Chesney since that last fateful encounter, nor did she expect to do so, even though she knew he had received an invitation. This in no way lessened the feeling of longing and desolation that weighed on her heart as he failed to come.

Dysart stood up with her to open the ball. He proved to be an excellent dancer, but she would have preferred Ches as a partner, even if he had stepped on her toes.

The earl noticed her downcast expression and hugged her briefly during a cross-hand twirl. "Chin up, luv, we'll yet live through this." He looked her over approvingly. "Yes indeed, quite passable."

She gave him a weak smile. He really was very nice, and quite dashing with a crown on his golden curls, an ermine trimmed cape and a sword by his side. When Bella suggested that he go costumed as Parsifal, the shocked aunts had turned pale.

"Never!" Lady Almeria had exclaimed. "The Old Gentleman might take it as an insult that anyone would think of stepping into his shoes while he still remained earthbound."

They had finally decided on King Arthur and Lady Guinevere, gowning Bella in the tall pointed hat, wimple, flowing robe and coronet of a medieval princess.

"And so appropriate," Dysart murmured in her ear. "I as Arthur by your side, when you really long for your Lancelot."

Dysart was searching among the other couples as they danced and wondered aloud where Mrs. Montfort could be.

"Mrs. Montfort! I hardly think a card was sent to her."

"Oh, she got one," Dysart said easily. "I saw to that. Full moon, you know. For our seance."

The movement of the dance separated them, and Bella stared after him. After the scene with Ches, all thought of Parsifal's treasure had fled from her mind. But to bring that woman here to her ball!

She pounced on Dysart when they came together again. "Have you considered what your aunts will say?"

The earl shrugged carelessly. "How would they discover her? All are masked and we shall away at midnight."

The dance ended and she curtsied automatically. "But that is when the announcement is to be made."

"I know." He grinned wickedly. "But I've no desire to appear a bobbing-block. The notice will have to appear in the normal manner on the pages of the *Morning Post*."

Before she could argue the point, which she had no real desire to do, the Duke of Devron appeared at her side, claiming her as partner in the next set. In the powdered wig and velvets of George III in court dress, he resembled the Regent more than ever. How could Ches ever have considered him a suitable suitor?

He bowed over her hand with surprising grace, and his bulging eyes twinkled up at her.

"I understand I am to wish you happy." He beamed, not at all upset to be cut from the running. So much for her fatal charms!

"But how did you know?" she asked. "It has not yet been announced."

He waggled a finger at her, chiding. "Can you wonder? Domestics have ears as well as do walls. Such a delightful secret is not meant to be kept. My valet informed me of it this morning."

He led her into the set just forming, still chuckling at his long-headedness. For the first time, Bella became conscious of the smiles and knowing looks of the others, feeling herself flush to be the centre of so much attention. It was so wrong! Somehow, the fact that everyone must know brought home the reality of a marriage to *Dysart,* not to Chesney.

*Oh, why did Ches not come?* But what did she expect from him? That he would cast off the tenets of a lifetime and charge in like Lochinvar to carry her off in the nick of time? No. Not noble, honourable Chesney Carlyle. *You are a fool,* she told herself. *A fool!*

But she kept watching the doors as the hour grew near to midnight.

Thus it was that she was the first to see the entrance of the figure in a Parsifal costume at thirteen minutes to twelve. It seemed not quite right, slightly blurred about the edges, but Bella blamed this on the champagne punch and effects of the dizzying twirls of the dance. Several minutes passed before she realized it was really the Old Gentleman who mingled among the costumed guests, not at all out of place in his Elizabethan garb, though not quite solid. He trod in a stately manner across the ballroom floor, towards the western wall.

Lady Almeria and Lady Eg had seen him and were clutching each other. Bella left Devron standing on the dance floor and ran to their side.

"Suppose he walks *through* someone!" she whispered. "Is there anything we can do before everyone panics?"

The aunts had already panicked and shook their heads, dumb with shock. The worst was yet to come.

Creswell announced a late guest, and a second Parsifal entered the room.

"It's Eustace!" Lady Almeria managed to gasp.

Bella grabbed her arm. Surely that was the same costume worn by the false Parsifal who attacked Dysart in the night. Even from a short distance she could see a clumsily repaired rip in the skirt of his doublet.

"That's the man!" she exclaimed. "He's the one who attacked Dysart!"

"*Eustace* attacked him? Oh, dear," Lady Almeria wailed. "If he has tried to harm Dysart, the Old Gentleman will be furious! He'll do something dreadful!" She pushed her sister forward. "Quick, Eg, get to Eustace and warn him."

Lady Eg started off, but before she caught up with Thorpington, a Sir Walter Raleigh entered the ballroom.

It was Chesney Carlyle, and he escorted a Queen Elizabeth with an unforgettable crown of burnished copper curls. In her arms, she carried a pug dog. Attila.

Bella saw only Ches. Their eyes met across the room, and her knees went weak with longing.

Lady Eg saw only his companion, and her reaction was quite different. Here was her chance to meet that woman and her magnificent dog! Just when she had become reconciled to falling back upon a distinctly inferior sire! Thorpington forgotten, she barged through the dancers towards that one and only dog.

She never made it. Her change of direction granted the Spectre of Spadefield an unobstructed view of Eustace Thorpington.

The two Parsifals met face to face in the centre of the floor, and a roll of thunder shook the air. Sheet lightning blasted the room. A whirlwind whipped one of the festooned paper garlands across the blazing candles in the centre chandelier and it exploded into flames. A fireball burn of the bolt of lightning raced down the garland to the artificial palm which tethered it, and blasted through the western wall. One of the Parsifals vanished in a thunderclap.

Pandemonium broke loose. Guests fled in terror amid screams of "Fire!" The smoke-filled ballroom emptied as though the spigot were knocked from a barrel of ale. Dysart herded his transfixed aunts out the door. Mrs. Montfort stood clutching Attila, stunned.

"Come, Izzy, hurry!" Ches yelled, steering widow and dog ahead of him.

Bella hesitated. Eustace Thorpington sat in the middle of the floor, his mouth opening and closing. Spectral blue flames danced from hair that stood on end in spiky tufts.

She seized the punchbowl from the refreshment table and dashed the contents over his head, dousing him. The wraith-fire in the chandelier went out as magically as it had begun. The sudden silence seemed to beat against her ears.

The aunts crept back into the ballroom and gazed down on the shell of Eustace Thorpington, who still sat on the floor mumbling, his head steaming like a pot on the boil.

"He asked for it," said Lady Almeria at last. Her feathers were sadly ruffled, and she knew whom to blame. "That addlepate!" She turned to Bella. "Do you know what they are saying outside? A common fire! Blaming the paper garlands and the candles in the chandelier!"

"Yes," said Eg. "I heard one man say some idiot must have opened a window and created a draft."

"Can you countenance such stupidity?" Lady Almeria noticed that Bella still held the empty punchbowl. "Put that down, my dear. He's beyond help, thank goodness. Do you know, only one guest had the intelligence to recognize the Spectre of Spadefield, a delightful lady with the loveliest red hair."

"I suppose," Lady Eg muttered hopelessly, "she was carrying away a pug dog."

"I didn't notice," said Almeria.

Dysart returned, followed by two members of the Watch, come to investigate the commotion. The excitement, he informed the men, was over. "I sent everyone home," he told his aunts. "I said there was too much damage to continue our ball."

Thorpington was led away by the Watch, no doubt to Bedlam. The aunts, exhausted by the dramatic end to their party, retired to their chambers. Dysart and Bella were left, examining the wall damaged by the fireball.

They were joined unexpectedly by Fanny Montfort and Attila, followed by a harassed Chesney Carlyle.

"She won't go home," he apologized. "I tried."

"Of course I won't go home!" said the widow, giving Chesney a contemptuous glance. "What, leave the most incredible happening of my entire life? A genuine spectre! I don't believe I shall ever go home." She pushed Bella out of the way and studied the hole in the scorched panelling. "This is where he went.... Was ever there anything so exciting!"

The hole was about a foot across, its blackened edges still smoking. Inside was a sort of latch. Bella reached past Mrs. Montfort and gave it a lift.

The entire section of panelling scraped eerily against the stone behind it and moved aside, revealing an empty space, rather like a priest-hole. They crowded together, peering in. The little room was a landing for a narrow flight of steps that led upwards inside the six-foot-thick wall of the tower.

"By God!" Dysart cried, catching Bella up in his arms and hugging her. "The secret passage! I've been searching for this ever since I was out of leading strings."

The strange sound Bella heard behind her came from Chesney, grinding his teeth. She hastily shoved Dysart away when she saw Ches's clenched fists.

"But your family must have known about this!" she exclaimed. "Even Eustace has discovered it. Why did no one tell you?"

"I expect it was because my father died when I was very young. He'd have shown it to me, but he was something of a Tartar and no doubt did not hold with children creeping about between the walls and jumping out of panels at his guests." He was inside the little room, peering up the dark steps. "Come on, let's see where they lead. Get me a candle."

Bella snatched one of the tapers from a wall sconce and handed it to him and went back for one for herself. The delay put her at the end of the line. Dysart, Ches and the widow, with Attila scrambling after them, were already ascending.

The staircase was less than two feet wide, running straight up within the tower wall, behind the spiral steps they had climbed before. The stairs were so steep, and the treads so narrow, that the broad-shouldered men—and the widow—were forced to mount them like crabs. Outmanoeuvred, Bella followed behind.

She trembled with anticipation, never doubting that this was the moment. They were about to find Parsifal's treasure at last. Oh, why couldn't that widow move faster?

Dysart had reached the top. A solid wall faced him. He gave a tentative push, and it swung outward on well-oiled hinges. They crowded after him, bursting through a hidden niche by one of the house chimneys and out onto the roof of the tower.

"Eustace." Dysart fairly snarled the name. "This explains these unnatural sightings of late. He's been prowling about at night, searching the place for Parsifal's hoard. I'm glad the Old Gentleman found him," he added grimly.

Bella looked around. The roof was absolutely bare, edged by a crenelated wall. Dawn was breaking. The view of London was magnificent, but it failed to include a treasure.

"I was so sure," Bella wailed, as they trailed back down the perilous steps to the secret room by the ballroom. "I thought we *must* have found your fortune."

Dysart threw his free arm about her shoulders, giving her a comforting squeeze. "Never mind, luv. I didn't believe it was here. Parsifal was a Westphale, remember. He'd never leave blunt behind."

"But, Dysart, he *led* me here. I know he did." She blinked rapidly, but a tear trickled down her cheek.

The earl, who had fallen quite into the habit of kissing her, tipped up her face and did so.

"Hoy!" yelled Chesney, driven beyond endurance. Hugging was one thing, but this was too much. His love, his frustration, his despair—and the champagne punch he'd been drinking to drown them—quite went to his head. He yanked his costume sword from its scabbard. "Take your filthy hands off her!"

Dysart looked at his hands. They were indeed dirt streaked from the ancient stones of the staircasing and had left prints on her fancy costume.

"Sorry, luv," he said.

An apology was not enough. Striking a fencing stance, Ches shouted the traditional swordsman's challenge. "Sa-sa!"

Dysart's outfit had come with a sword as well, and he was never one to resist a lark. He handed his candle to Bella and steel rang on steel. Attila the pug, yapping with delight, bounded into the battle, biting ankles indiscriminately.

Fanny Montfort screamed. "Stop! You will step on him!"

"What?" Dysart asked, lowering his rapier.

Ches, on the point of spitting him, tried to check his lunge in midstride and tripped over the dog. He cannoned into Fanny, who had dived in to rescue Attila, and she crashed against the side wall of the secret room.

With the teeth-jarring scrape of ancient wood on rough stone, a new panel slid away beneath her substantial weight. With a shriek, she fell backwards down another flight of the narrow stairs, bumping from one to the next to a cellar below.

Dysart plunged after her with a wild yell. Ches grabbed the earl's candle from Bella's hand and dashed after him. Bringing her own candle, Bella followed anxiously, praying the widow was not badly hurt.

Fanny Montfort lay at the foot of the steps, in the midst of a decayed leather bag that had split open, scattering a glittering array of jewels and gold across the floor of the tiny cellar.

Beside her lay the skeleton of a short man dressed in scraps of mouldering velvet, a too-long sword entangled between its leg bones.

Dysart ignored everything but Fanny. He seized her shoulders, shaking her as Ches had Bella. "Fanny, don't be dead!" he begged.

She sat up and sorted herself out. "Where is Attila?" she asked.

"To the devil with Attila," Dysart cried. "Fan, my love—are you hurt?"

She picked up a fabulous emerald necklace and turned it about, awestruck. It glittered in the light of the candles. "Nothing," she declared, "that one of these will not cure."

Oblivious to the sparkling treasure, Dysart kicked aside a heap of jewels and swept her into his arms.

"Anything, my dearest Fan. Only say that you will marry me."

A great and lasting love shone in the widow's glowing eyes as she gazed at the wondrous gems. "Certainly," she said, and was enveloped in a passionate embrace.

Chesney looked at the pair thoughtfully. "Bella, my dear, I collect my betrothal is at an end."

"As is mine!" she exclaimed. "The aunts no longer need my fortune and—oh, Ches, I do love you so."

Chesney carefully stuck his candle on the floor in a puddle of melted wax and took Bella's candle from her and set it on the other side. He turned and held out his arms. Bella threw herself into them and he demonstrated that although he might not be a gazetted rake, he was quite as adept as Dysart in claiming his woman.

A long time later, leaving the earl and his Fan seated on the stone floor gleefully sorting jewelled tiaras, parures, rings, bracelets and brooches from golden chains and tarnished silver, Ches and Bella departed.

Lost in the wonder of their happy ending and blissfully unaware of any but each other, they climbed hand in hand up the secret staircase to the ballroom. On the top step sat a nebulous cloud, smelling of acrid smoke. The apparition seemed to be wearing an Elizabethan ruff and holding a too-long sword on his lap. As they passed through him Parsifal smiled, complacent at last.

Attila, ignored and forgotten, explored Spadefield House. Lady Eg was lying awake, sighing over her missed opportunity, when she heard a snuffling and scuffing from the corridor outside her chamber. Curious, she crawled out of bed and peeked through a crack in her door. The dawning of a dream come true spread over her chubby face.

Opening her portal wide, she shoved Melisande out into the hall.

# ROMANCE IS A YEARLONG EVENT!

Celebrate the most romantic day of the year with MY VALENTINE! (February)

CRYSTAL CREEK
When you come for a visit Texas-style, you won't want to leave! (March)

Celebrate the joy, excitement and adjustment that comes with being JUST MARRIED! (April)

Go back in time and discover the West as it was meant to be...UNTAMED—Maverick Hearts! (July)

LINGERING SHADOWS
*New York Times* bestselling author Penny Jordan brings you her latest blockbuster. Don't miss it! (August)

BACK BY POPULAR DEMAND!!!
Calloway Corners, involving stories of four sisters coping with family, business and romance! (September)

FRIENDS, FAMILIES, LOVERS
Join us for these heartwarming love stories that evoke memories of family and friends. (October)

Capture the magic and romance of Christmas past with HARLEQUIN HISTORICAL CHRISTMAS STORIES! (November)

## WATCH FOR FURTHER DETAILS IN ALL HARLEQUIN BOOKS!

CALEND